The Conga Player's Dues

A Novel

By

Wig Nelson

ISBN-10 98331442X
ISBN-13 9780983314424

Xeries Press

If only you and two other people knew that the destruction of your beloved planet was imminent and nearly upon you, would you tell anyone about it? Neither would I . . .

Also By Wig Nelson

Sirens

The Psychic

Jacks and Hands

Tall Tales Long & Short

Tall Tales Long & Short II

Starry Night

A Feeling of Power
The Musical

The Little Shop of Lyrics
A Workshop

CDs By Wig Nelson

Fire and Life

Get There

Wigged Out

Fools You Bet On

A Feeling of Power
The Musical

The Little Shop of Lyrics
An Audio Book

This book is dedicated to you, the reader, who is the reason for all of literature. I don't need to write the stories down for my own benefit. Like my protagonist, Mack Willis, I have an eidetic memory. I sincerely wish that I did not.

- Wig Nelson

The Conga Player's Dues

Part One

Mason's Laser

Prologue

I've been told that 99.9 percent of everything everywhere is dark matter. That's pretty hard to believe when you're at the beach in Florida at high noon on a summer day. It seems awfully bright to me. But that's just the illusion created by perspective. This whole planet is really a minor player in the eternal production called "being." We just happen to live on a rock that revolves around one of the many trillion insignificant points of light. For the most part, it's really dark out there.

Our most egregious misconception, however, is assuming that it's really quiet out there as well. For years, scientists were looking at all the other insignificant points of light hoping to hear someone talk back to us in some kind of mathematical blather. It's really strange to finally know the truth. It's a little bit scary, a little more sad, but most of all strange. To finally get the message that for eons has been falling on deaf ears as well as blind eyes, it took Mason's laser to deliver that message to us. All of the telescopes on the summit of Mauna Kea couldn't hear the message. They can only measure whole photons. Who could imagine that dark matter has been screaming at us all along, *half a photon at a time.*

Chapter One

I was trying to give the incessantly jabbering woman the impression that I had dozed off. Unfortunately, she wasn't buying it. She went on and on about her new grandchild (her fifth) that she had just seen for the first time in Orlando, Florida. She talked about all the cute expressions little Carolyn had at such a remarkably young age. She was surprised at how the baby would smile at her (she was sure it wasn't gas) constantly. It seemed to me that this woman thought that she was the first grandmother on Earth, and she just couldn't wait to break the news. Didn't she know how excruciatingly boring she was? Had she no clue? Sure, the baby is cute. All babies are cute to someone for God's sake. So what? Okay, the kid has blue eyes and lots of hair already - big deal.

She's got her mother's lips (which is *sooooo* fortunate because she just happens to be a lip model – she also does hand jobs from time to time - *Hand jobs?*) and her father's nose. If the woman could just hear herself for one minute, she would be falling all over herself with apologies and promises to be quiet for the remainder of the train ride. We were almost to New Jersey, and she started in about the freaking grandchild somewhere around the Chesapeake Bay Bridge. Maybe there really isn't a God. Or maybe there is and yours truly, Mack Willis, was really bad – and then he died – and this is hell. Forget the devil, for Christ's sake. Nobody could make me suffer any worse than this old bag.

But it really wasn't as bad as I was making it seem, was it? I caught myself and swam back up through my ocean of cynicism and surfaced just long enough to open my eyes briefly and smile at the woman. That was a mistake, I knew it at once. It only encouraged her. Next time I would fly from Florida to New Jersey, the hell with the train. *The train ride from hell.*

"Are you a musician?" she asked motioning to the conga drums that were sticking out of the overhead compartment.

No, I'm a drum salesman, I almost said. Instead I just nodded and turned away making a point to take in the view of the countryside whizzing by. She didn't get the hint, naturally.

"I used to play the accordion," she offered. "Have you ever played with an accordionist?"

I just looked at her for a long moment and then finally said, "Not that I can recall."

"There, you see? That's the problem, isn't it?" she said. "It's usually just a solo instrument. In a way, I'm kind of sorry that I didn't move on to piano or something."

I'm sorry, too, I thought. She continued, naturally, "When I think of all the money that my parents spent on the lessons and instruments themselves, (she had three in her illustrious career) I can't help but feel a little bit guilty. Now I don't play at all, and I can't think of what to do with my accordion."

I've got a suggestion.

"Such a waste," she finally concluded.

You won't get any argument from me, lady. I felt the hairs rise on the back of my neck for about the fifth time during the trip. I got the spooky feeling again that someone was watching me. I ignored the woman and turned back around and looked through the car. The same people stared back at me with the same sleepy expressions. *Lucky bastards,* I thought to myself. *I wish I could sleep.* I had a hard time sleeping in my own bed, let alone in a rocking coach car suffering some blabbermouth. Maybe New Jersey would be different. The cooler night air might help. Plus, with any luck, I had left Joey Berio miles behind me. No sign of him yet. So far, so good. I scolded myself for the fiftieth time for ever getting involved with a bunch of goombahs. What was I thinking for God's sake? Nobody ever gets out clean. *Stupido!*

"Are you looking for someone?" asked the woman.

"I hope not," I said absently.

"I beg your pardon?" she asked.

"No, not really."

"It's just that you keep turning around as though you expect to see someone that you know. Were you meeting someone in Baltimore?" she asked.

"No. Why Baltimore?" I asked her.

"That was the last stop," she said.

"Oh. No, I was just looking to see if there was anyone I knew on the train."

"And is there?" she asked.

"Nope."

"Well, I'm glad that we got this chance to get to know each other."

I'm not.

"But I really don't know all that much about you," she continued. "I suppose I've been doing most of the talking."

No, not you.

"All I really know is that you're a musician. Are you coming to New Jersey for one of your gigs?" she giggled.

"As a matter of fact, I am."

"You're a professional, then."

"No, not really. I'm just filling in for someone in my brother-in-law's band."

"Are they famous?" she asked hopefully.

"Not until I get there," I said sarcastically.

"You must be very good," she said - her expression speaking volumes of her obvious disbelief. She was starting to give me a reason to dislike her other than the fact that she *Just Couldn't Keep Her Mouth Shut!*

"I try," I said marveling at my self control.

"Why don't you tell me about yourself, are you married? Any kids?"

"Nope. No wife. No kids."

"Have you got a girlfriend?"

Jesus this is getting weird. Now we're getting to be old friends. She's like some aunt that pinches your cheek, never even dreaming that it hurts like hell every time she does it. I could see that we were almost to the Delaware Water Gap, and the train was just a few minutes out of Clinton, so what the hell, I let fly, "Well, I'll tell you, but don't say you didn't ask for it. My name, as you know, is Mack. It stands for Mackenzie Willis. I'm an amateur musician on my way to join the band *Blue Cactus*. I'm recently divorced from a woman named Susan, who in many ways is a real ball-buster. I'm a professional private investigator and ex-homicide investigator. I recently took a job for a woman who's married to the mob, but that's okay because she was also born into it. Her name is Sophia Dimiccia, and she hired me to take pictures of her husband screwing around, but it gets even better. She also wanted me to take pictures of her husband beating her during their own screwing around, but that's okay, according to the husband, Carmen, because he claims it's the only way she can have a decent orgasm. Are you with me so far?" I asked, certain that I had gone *too* far, but the woman said, "Oh, yes."

"So Carmen finds out about the pictures, and he's none too pleased with yours truly, as you can imagine. He sends one of his *acquaintances* named Joey, *"The Ice Pick,"* Berio, to explain to me my options for continuing to breathe in and out, if you catch my drift. Well, my mother didn't raise any suicides, so I told him I understand completely and couldn't agree with him more. I'll delete the pictures faster than you can say, *"cement overshoes,"* but does that get me off the hook? Not on your life *or mine for that matter.*

Into the picture comes Sophia's daddy, Frankie DeLucca, who's an even bigger and badder wise guy than Carmen Dimiccia. Well, daddy says his little girl trusted me to do a very important service for her, which can't be repeated since Carmen is wise to the picture and will make damn sure that he no longer appears in any. Daddy says if she doesn't get the pictures, again I might find it difficult with the breathing in and breathing out. Get the picture?"

"Yes," said the woman. "I think it's fascinating. Do go on."

"Well, I'm glad you think it's fascinating because I think it just plain sucks. I'm stuck in the middle, but that's not the worst of it, then there's also Susan."

"Your wife," said the woman.

"Ex-wife and secretary. Naturally, she knows about the job and she's siding with Sophia because she doesn't believe Carmen's story that she likes the rough sex. All Susan can see is the abuse angle. She thinks I'm a coward for not standing up to Carmen, which by the way I am, but that's not the real reason. Carmen threatened to kill Susan, not me, if Sophia and her daddy get their hands on the pictures.

So I've got Susan on the one hand berating me day in and day out for abandoning the poor little victim of domestic violence and two goombahs on the other - just waiting for me to make one move or the other so they can snuff me. Susan and I decided to make a break, but she still works for me because I still need her services, and it's the only way I can afford to pay her alimony. Believe me it's a mess. All of a sudden, I decided that a trip to New Jersey might be the best thing for my health. How's that?" I asked the woman.

"I would imagine that after all that, playing the drums might seem a little dull."

"One can only hope."

"Oh, look," she said. "I think we're pulling into the station."

"It's about time," I said. "I don't really like to travel as you can tell."

"And here I was boring you with all of my stories," said the woman, "but you probably weren't even listening, not that I can blame you."

"Not listening? Well, maybe not, but *hearing* I can assure you."

"I'm not sure that I understand the difference," said the woman.

"Well, then I'll tell you. Your husband's name is Franklyn. He's sixty-four and had an ulcer but he's dealing with it. He's let you change his diet. I won't bore you with what he's eating, but trust me I know. You have three kids, Billy, Sean and Claire. Billy's married to Jennifer and Sean to Colleen. Claire's still single; she's in college at Auburn in Georgia and doesn't come home enough to Westfield, New Jersey, where you and Franklyn have a four bedroom house that's too big for your needs. Billy and Jennifer live in Orlando, Florida. They're the one with the newborn, Carolyn, who's seven weeks old yesterday. It's their third child because they already have Cory and Dana.

Sean and Colleen live in Houston and have the twins, Charlie and Mary. You were a nurse having gone to St. Luke's in New York City, which is where you met Franklyn. He's in obstetrics and just about to retire, but decided not to make the trip with you to Orlando because he was told by his golf buddy, Dr. Marvin Shapiro, to check in to Sloan Kettering for some follow up tests on his stomach problems. Did I leave anything out?"

The woman just sat there looking at me for some time. I suppose I shouldn't have messed with her mind like that, but I thought she had it coming. The conductor called, "Clinton. Clinton, New Jersey. Next stop, Newark, and then Westfield. Clinton...Clin..."

"Well, I guess this is where I get off," I said. "Give my best to Franklyn, and don't worry about little Charlie. A lot of kids stutter when they're young, but they get over it. Take it easy, Mrs. Jones."

~

Mason was late meeting me at the Clinton, New Jersey, train station, but it wasn't the first time he'd let me down. I felt somewhat out of place standing on the platform with my conga drums as if I were a street musician who, for some reason or another, decided to stop playing. The problem is that I don't have carry-bags for them, so I just set them in their stand next to me when I travel. I was supposed to gig with Mason's band *Blue Cactus* for about three weeks. Their drummer, Mitch, had to go to Texas for an indeterminate amount of time because his mother's health was failing pretty quickly, and he didn't know how much time she had left.

I looked around expecting to see Carmen Dimiccia or one of his goons. I thought I left Florida pretty cleanly, but *you never let your guard down if you want to grow old,* I told myself.

All paranoia aside, I could have sworn that I'd seen this guy named Joey Berio at the train station in Orlando. He works for Dimiccia, and I'm pretty sure he doesn't cut his lawn or anything like that. His nickname is *"The Ice Pick,"* but I don't think he's a bartender either. Man, I *knew* I was getting spooked. I'd been a P.I. one case too long. Sometimes I think it's better to get whacked and get it over with than to get spooked. Almost better, anyway.

The job I was supposed to do for Dimiccia's wife, Sophia, got too complicated. Especially the part about him choking her during sex. I wasn't sure whether to snap the shutter or call 911. I decided to just beg out of the whole situation, but nobody wants to let go.

Carmen says he'll snuff me if Sophia gets the pic's – Sophia says her daddy, Frankie DeLucca, will snuff me if she doesn't get them – Berio says his obligations to Dimiccia go beyond the grave, *whatever the hell that means* – it's a mess. Long story short – I needed to reinvent my life in a big way as soon as possible.

"Excuse me, sir," said a hostile voice behind me. I turned around and saw this woman with a scarf around her head and a five o'clock shadow glaring at me, "Those drums of yours are blocking the landing."

"I'm sorry, lady. I'm just looking for my ride."

"Well, stand off to the side," she barked at me.

I'm not a professional musician by the way, and neither is Mason nor are any members of his band. Believe it or not they are all chemical engineers. Their sound is a little rough around the edges, but no worse than the majority of club bands that bang out classic rock cover tunes in smoky rooms across the country.

You know the kind of places I mean: the tables are dusty, the waitress has a few tattoos and a slight limp, and the only place your shoes don't stick to the ground is on the dance floor. Mason hates places like that, especially the smoke. His contacts start to burn, and the smell kind of sickens him until he has to rush outside to get some fresh air in his lungs. But he does it for the music. Mason loves classic rock, and he does a fair rendition of Black Magic Woman on his Gibson-Les Paul.

Forgive me if I digress - I was telling you that I'm not a professional musician when I got sidetracked. I'm a private investigator from Deerfield Beach, Florida, who just happens to play the conga drums. My wife Susan had recently left me, but her haunting accusations just refused to fade like a stray cat that won't take no for an answer.

I can still hear the implication of my cowardice in her voice, "*I can't believe you intend to turn your back on that poor girl.*"

"*Susan, please!*" I begged her.

"*Dimiccia beats her, Mack. I don't suppose that means anything to you, does it?*"

"*He says that she likes it when he chokes her. He says that's the only way she can get a nut.*"

"*Oh, pul-ease, Mack. I suppose the bruises on her face are foreplay.*"

"*I don't know what they are,*" I told her. "*I've destroyed the pictures,*" I lied.

"*Sophia's father is a man, even if you aren't. Frankie DeLucca can protect you. That's what you're afraid of, isn't it? You're afraid that someone might beat you up. Meanwhile you let that girl get beaten up day after day by that monster. How can you live with yourself, Mack?*"

I should have sent the pictures. Nothing would have happened to me. Dimiccia made it clear when he asked me, "*How's your wife, Mack. How's Susan. She doin' okay?*"
I got the picture all right. That's why Sophia never got hers. Dimiccia was specific when he told me, "*Susan's next, Mack.*"

Mason lives in New Jersey where he works for Bell Labs. He's married to my sister, Billie, who used to sing with the band until she got a bad case of nodes on her vocal chords. She can still do studio work if she wants to, but she doesn't have the volume anymore. Being a torch singer, as in *blow-torch*, can be pretty tough on the pipes. Anyway, Mason said while Mitch is away the band agreed to having only congas and a tambourine if I wanted to fill in. Since my caseload is just about clear, I decided to give it a try.

Some guy threw a dollar bill down on the pavement next to me so I had to tell him, "I'm not working here, man. I just don't have any travel bags." He never even turned around, so I picked up the dollar. Just as I was rising, a young, dark-haired woman grabbed me rather firmly by the elbow. She was dressed in sneakers and jeans beneath a Navy P-coat, which seemed like a lot of clothing for September in New Jersey. She pressed a dollar into my hand and said, "Tell her she was right."

"What did you say?" I asked her looking for Joey Berio.

"Not here," she said. "We're being watched."

Oh, Jesus, already? I thought looking around me. I noticed that the woman had very shiny, dark hair and a lazy eye. It made her look kind of interesting. I always wonder which one is looking at me when I see people like that. *No wonder I moved away from here. These people are still nuts. Not much has changed in fifteen years.* I couldn't help wondering what the hell she was   talking about. *Tell who she was right? Susan? Where the hell is Mason?* I wondered. *He's probably at the lab or something and   totally forgot that he was supposed to pick me up. I guess I could get a cab, but it'll cost me an arm and a leg.*

All of a sudden I saw the woman go down. She dropped like a stone to the pavement and banged her head slightly against a garbage can. I knelt down next to her to see if I could help. She had her hand against her neck like she had just swatted a mosquito, and when she took it away there was a small puddle of brown viscous fluid like molasses where her hand had been. When she looked at her hand, she began to cry and shake her head saying, "Oh no, it's not fair!"

"What's not fair?" I asked her.

"God damn it! A fucking ice dart," she mumbled. "Probably cyanide or curare. Life sucks and then it's over," she said in tears.

"Do you need an ambulance?" I asked lamely. I couldn't see anything wrong with her except for the brown liquid on her neck. It looked like she'd squished a bug.

"It's too late," she said. "You're here for Blue Cactus, aren't you?"

"Excuse me?" I asked. She really had me confused then.

"You're Willis, right?"

"That's right," I said. "But how did you. . ."

"It doesn't matter," she cried, and then coughed weakly, and I noticed a small drop of blood from her nose fall to the pavement. She sniffled and said, "Tell Martie . . . tell her she was right about him. He shared a cab with Dimi. . .," and then she passed out. Right there before me she was gone in an instant. One minute I'm talking to her about an ambulance and the next she's gone. Her eyes glassed over and a woman behind me cried, "Someone call a cop. I think he killed her."

The first thing I thought was Dimi . . .? Did she mean Dimiccia? *Holy shit,* I thought. *They're here.*

I got to my feet and said, "Call an ambulance. This woman has passed out, and I'm not getting a pulse."

"Are you a doctor?" someone asked.

"No." I said. "I'm pretty sure it's too late for that."

"What did you do to her?" the woman asked me.

"Nothing. I swear I was just standing next to her and she passed out. Who's calling 911?" I asked. "My cell phone won't work here," I told them. Then I spotted Mason and called out to him, "Mason, over here. Do you have your cell phone?"

"I've already called," said the woman. "The police are on the way."

"I'm gonna' start CPR, Mason. Will you help?"

"Sure," he said. "Go, man."

"Okay, fifteen and two, got it?"

"Go," he said.

I loosened her collar and began thrusting on her sternum to a count of fifteen. Then Mason pulled her head back and pinched off her nose to give her two breaths. Then it was fifteen pulses again, but we still couldn't get a pulse. The woman with the cell phone began to cry. We continued on to no avail until the paramedics arrived about five minutes later. She was gone. They tried the defibrillator paddles, but it was too late.

"Must have been a massive coronary," suggested one of the EMT's. "She a friend of yours?" he asked me.

"Never saw her before in my life," I told him.

About a half-hour later we were in Mason's Lexus driving from the train station toward his home in the hills of Hunterden County.

"Man that was weird," he said. "You ever see anyone die like that before?" he asked, and then I could see that he was immediately sorry. He added, "I meant outside of work."

"Nope. Did you notice how she was dressed?"

"Yeah, heavy coat, sneakers, jeans, what about it?"

"Did you see what was under the coat?" I asked him.

"What are you talking about, Mack?"

"She was wearing Kevlar."

"Jesus. Are you sure?"

"I know Kevlar when I see it, Mason."

"Yeah, I guess you do."

"You want to hear the kicker?"

"What?"

"She knew who I was. *And* she mentioned the name Blue Cactus."

"Bullshit," said Mason.

"Why would I make that up?"

"We're not that popular, man. Nobody knows us."

"She did."

"Damn. I guess we just lost a fan."

"That's not very funny, Mason."

"I know, I was only kidding. I'm sorry as hell that the woman died. You think she had a heart attack?"

"No."

"Me neither. Cops take your name?"

"Yup."

"Did they say don't leave town, the whole bit?"

"No. They know I had nothing to do with it. Let me ask you something. You ever hear of an ice dart?"

"Jesus! What are you saying?" he asked.

"I'm not really sure. It's just something that she said. She wasn't making much sense. She said, '*A fucking ice dart. Cyanide or curare.*'"

"I've never heard of an ice dart, and I don't even want to know what the hell it is. Did you bring any trouble with you from Florida, Mack?"

"Hell, no," I lied. I was starting to get spooked. "Nice state you've got here, Mason. I'm here for ten minutes and somebody gets whacked."

"I guess there's no crime in Florida, right, Mack."

"Who is Marty?" I asked him.

"What?" he asked.

"The woman at the station said, *'Tell Marty she was right about him. He shared a cab with Dimi.'*"

"Did you mention that to the cops?" he asked me.

"No, why?"

"Good. Just forget what you heard." Mason tried to change the subject, "So besides all the commotion at the station, how was your trip?"

"What do you mean, how was my trip? Why the hell was that woman killed at the train station, Mason?"

"It doesn't concern you, Mack. I've got to ask you to drop it, okay?"

"I feel like getting back on the train," I told him.

"Take it easy, Mack. It's all over, man. You're here to gig with the band, that's all."

"Somehow I don't feel in the mood to play."

"Mack," he pleaded.

That's my name, Mack Willis. My sister was Billie Willis before she became Mrs. Mason Spender. I noticed that Mason hadn't shaved so I figured he hadn't been to work, but then again, who could tell with those egghead types?

"So, tell me. How was your trip?" he asked.

"It was okay," I said. "Trains are cool. You can sleep and stuff," I lied. *Never got a wink of sleep.*

"You ever think about getting some travel cases for those?" he asked motioning toward the drums in the back seat. "Then you could check them on an airplane."

"I've thought about it," I said. "I don't use them very often, and you know how I hate to travel."

"You still afraid to fly?" he asked me.

"That's a crock of shit and you know it," I told him. "I just prefer trains, that's all."

"Uh huh."

"Why would I be afraid of flying?"

"I don't know. It's just something that Billie said one time."

"It wouldn't be the first time she read me wrong."

"I guess she just gets a little pissed because you're hip to her tricks," said Mason.

"She sleeping?" I asked.

"Like a baby."

"What about the pills?" I asked.

"What about them?" he said. "Listen, I really appreciate you helping us out, Mack. How are the wrists?" he asked, like he was worried that I was gonna' stink up Carnegie Hall or something.

"They're loose enough," I told him and then added, "I'm not ready to play with *Carlos Santana,* but then again, neither is *Blue Cactus.*"

"We're getting better, Mack. Peter has a new keyboard and we're doing a lot of *Cold Play*."

"That sounds like fun," I said. "I really like some of their tunes. It's pretty heady sometimes. Right up your alley, I guess."

"I'm just a frustrated guitar player who has to work for a living."

"Right," I said. "And I'm just Thomas Magnum who traded his Ferrari for a set of conga drums."

"Good move."

Chapter Two

O n our way to Mason's house he asked me if we could stop off at the lab. "What are you working on now?" I asked.

"I'm trying to dope some glass," he said.

"They pay you to smoke dope?" I said with false disbelief.

"Very funny, Mack. I'm mixing different elements with glass. It's called "*doping*." The glass feeds down into a segregated funnel template, and it keeps the same ratio no matter how thin the wire."

"You lost me as usual," I said.

"I'm trying to make a wire out of glass."

"Really? I've never heard of that," I said.

"Oh, we do it all the time. You've seen fiber-optics, right?"

"Yeah," I told him. "But I thought they were made out of plastics. You know . . . polymers."

"They are, mostly, but there's a lot less energy loss with glass."

"So what's the practical application? How does it make money?" I asked.

"That's not my end of it, Mack. I just do the math so to speak, but I think it reduces the number of boosters needed for long range energy transfers."

"What? Are they expensive or something?" I asked.

"Haven't a clue," he told me. "But some of them are under water when the cable has to go across the ocean."

I was starting to get it, *I thought*. Transatlantic cables were extremely expensive, but I thought they were ancient history. I thought everything went up as in all the hundreds of satellites in space. Maybe that's because I had lived in Melbourne, Florida, for a while where every other week they were launching some damn thing or another. *So all this work and expense is to transfer information across long distances with a certain percent less energy loss. Right?* Something didn't seem to gel.

Information was already cruising along at about a billion miles an hour. Hell, my nephew, Jay played real time video games with some kid in *Australia*. I wasn't buying it. I figured this wouldn't be the first time that a scientist was unwittingly working on something that he wasn't entirely briefed about. Naturally, as a P.I., I suspected the worst. Human nature has shown me her ugly face once too often. I knew it was just a matter of time before I got out of the game or become one of the dark players. I've found   myself being tempted just a little too often lately. To look the other way - lose a few photographs for a quick ten-large, or as in the Sophia Dimiccia case - save somebody like Susan's ass.

Hell, I'm not Jesus Christ, so maybe playing the congas for a while might save what little there is left of Mack Willis. I still wasn't getting the glass wire thing, so I asked Mason, "This glass wire, is it brittle?"

"I don't think so. I've never really worked with much of the finished product," he said.

I believed him. Mason is the only person I know who can work on something for over a year and be totally oblivious to its impact on society as long as he has a fresh problem to solve. I wonder if Rosenberg had a fresh problem after developing the Atomic Bomb for the Manhattan Project? Anyway, I still wasn't getting the glass thing. I asked, "Mason, how come when you bend this piece of glass it doesn't break?"

"First of all, it's covered in a polymer shield for strength, and then it's covered again in a darker polymer that prohibits the loss of any light energy. The idea is to implode the light onto the core away from the cladding so the signal is accelerated to a plus-light threshold."

"Never mind," I said.

"No, it's not that difficult to understand. Look at it this way. What if glass had different properties relative to its core and its cladding?"

I just looked at him for a few seconds trying to figure out if he was goofing on me. Finally I said, "English, Mason. I didn't go to Berkeley."

"Okay. What if a tube of glass was smoky on the outside and clear on the inside? What would happen?"

"Light would travel more easily down the center," I said.

"Good," he said. "Now what if you doped the glass on the outside with germanium?" he asked me.

"Then you'd have lovely geraniums on the outside of your glass."

"Not geraniums, *germanium*," he said. "It's an element."

"What does it do?" I asked.

"It's a photo-retardant. It degenerates the intensity of the signal," he said.

"So how does that help you?" I asked.

"Well, if your core was just clear glass, it wouldn't. But what if you doped the core, the inside of the glass tube, with fluorine? Do you see it now?"

"Sure," I lied. I figured I'd asked enough stupid questions for one day.

"Man, it was really cool when I configured the first core," he said. "The cladding kept intruding and I couldn't maintain a clear barrier. So when it finally worked, I took a week off and went surfing in Barbados. My boss didn't say a thing."

"Good for you," I said. "I'd like to look at some of your set lists when we get to the house," I needed to be familiar with the songs the band was going to play in order to be worth a damn. I hadn't played music for some time, but I knew it would come back to me with a little practice. Chipping off the rust, we used to call it.

What I really missed was the trance-like automation. I used to reach a place of near euphoria by becoming one with the rhythms of the congas. It was music, yes, but it was also something more. In a selfish kind of sense, it became about centering my spirit. The song was secondary. What mattered was my spirit in the instant of expression.

Anyway, the instant of expression didn't pay the bills all that well, so I became a P.I. My return to music has been long overdue.

"I'll give you our set lists when we get to the house," said Mason. "I've even got some *Santana* you can listen to if you want."

"Might help," I said. "But some of those moves are way beyond me, man."

"Well, you can still keep a beat, can't you?"

"Don't worry about me, Mason. Worry about your souped-up phone cables."

"Oh, it's not just communications," said Mason. "It also has some laser applications."

"Lasers?" I asked.

Chapter Three

When we arrived at his lab, I noticed that Mason had his own parking space. I was surprised to see his name stenciled on the curb.

"Pretty snazzy," I told him.

"It's no big deal. There're twelve of us on a rotation. It's just my turn, that's all."

"They re-stencil the curb every month?" I asked.

"Pretty sharp, these detective types," he said sarcastically.

It was Saturday so there weren't many other cars in the lot, but I noticed a fair amount of upscale models. I couldn't help but mention, "These are some nice cars, Mason. I didn't know that lab work paid this well."

"We do all right," he said. "But it's the company that makes the real money. Remember when I developed that process to make fuel out of wood pulp?"

"Yeah, I remember. I thought you'd make a ton of money on that one."

"Works for hire, Pal," he said.

"What do you mean?" I asked him.

"When you work for a company and use their materials to develop a process, all rights belong to the company."

"That doesn't sound fair," I said.

"They pay me a nice salary plus benefits. Who's to say they wouldn't have gotten there without me? There were about six of us working on it at the time."

"Six scientists working on the same problem?" I asked.

"Sure," he said. "Sometimes more."

"Do you work together?"

"Not always, but sometimes. It depends how much research is needed."

"I can envision a bit of stiff competition among some of the scientists," I said as we were walking up to the side entrance to the lab. There was a card key slot beside the lock-set along with a keypad for entering a numeric code.

"Oh, it's a lot more mellow than you think. We help each other out sometimes when we have the time."

"Just one big happy family, right?" I asked.

"Something like that."

Mason inserted his card and punched in a four-digit code. The door swung inward and I heard a hissing noise, which was unmistakably an airlock seal bursting toward us.

"Come on," said Mason as he stepped through the doorway.

"Why the airlock," I asked.

"Part of this installation has a clean room for nano-technology grants."

"Refresh me," I said.

"Very small machines," he said as he waved to a uniformed guard standing by a lever on the inside of a second door fitted with a large glass panel. The guard gave Mason a thumbs-up signal and pulled on the lever. A second hissing noise erupted as the second door swung outward. Mason stepped inside the lab with me in tow like a faithful cocker spaniel. He said to the guard, "Hi, Bill. This is my brother-in-law, Mack."

"How's it going, Bill?" I asked extending my hand.

Bill Riley hesitated before shaking my hand, "Does he have a security clearance, Mason?" he asked with a concerned look on his face.

"Mack plays the congas, Bill. He's filling in for Mitch till he gets back."

"Cool," said Bill, "in that case, welcome aboard, Mack."

"I don't get it, Mason. What's going on?" I asked.

Both Mason and Bill started to laugh. Mason then said, "Bill manages the band. He's the manager of *Blue Cactus,*" he said laughing again.

"Ooh, tight security here. Everything's okay as long as you play with the band," I said incredulously. The two of them just started laughing again. I didn't quite get it. I guess it was an inside joke. I wasn't quite sure just what was so damned amusing. I said to Mason, "Why are we here, man? Just to meet Bill?"

"I have to check on something I've got cooking. It won't take too long. Come this way."

"Nice to meet you, Bill," I said as I followed Mason down a long hallway.

"I'll see you next Saturday, Mack," said Bill.

"What's next Saturday?" I asked Mason as we walked along. There were a series of large windows all down the hallway that allowed us to see into the labs, although some of them had sheets of white paper taped up to obscure them.

"We're playing a party. Actually, it's a *paid* gig. You'll love it."

"Oh, yeah? How come?" I asked sensing there was something more he wasn't telling me.

"It's at a really nice beach house in Bay Head."

"Cool," I said. "I haven't been there since I was a kid."

~

We arrived at a door to one of the labs and Mason had to use his card key again. I got the impression that the whole setup was not quite as casual as Mason liked to pretend. I could tell that these people took their security measures very seriously, even Bill.

I've had a few cases that involved corporate espionage, so I've learned the hard way not to underestimate the casual actions of technical personnel. They watch their backs constantly and sometimes err toward the side of paranoia.

When the lab door opened, one of the scientists shouted out, *"Wavemaster!"*

"Hey, Scott," said Mason. "When did *you* get here?"

"Man, I never left. Been here all night long."

"Right."

"I got here about an hour ago. What're *you* doing here?" asked Scott.

"Came to stir the sauce," said Mason.

"You should have called. I would have done it for you."

"If I like the segregation, I might press it today," said Mason.

"That was quick," said Scott. "What was it - half the time of beryllium?"

"Something like that," said Mason. I couldn't help but notice that his answer was a little vague. So much for sharing information and helping each other out. I asked Mason, "Is Scott in the band too?"

"No, way, man," said Scott. "I'm Scott Palmer, Mason's surfing buddy. Never learned to play an instrument."

"Mack Willis," I said extending my hand. "I play the congas."

"Good for you," said Scott. I couldn't help but detect a bit of condescension in his remark. I was just trying to make pleasant conversation, but it seemed like this one was a cold son-of-a-bitch.

"Mind if I watch you press," said Scott to Mason.

"It probably won't work. I've tried it before and the interface screwed up the cladding. It corrupted the signal in less than a hundred feet."

"They let you burn a hundred feet of product?" asked Scott. "You must be getting close to something."

"They were pissed when it didn't work. I won't get another shot unless the separation is flawless."

"Well, let's see how it looks," said Scott. "I'd love to watch you press something. I've been stuck on these laser rods for too long."

"You work on lasers?" I asked Scott.

"Yeah, mostly medical applications. R-K and shit like that. But they used one of my rods last year to make a cauterizing scalpel. That was cool."

"I don't like the looks of this bath," said Mason. "I think I cooled it too fast and now it's become corrupted. I don't think I want to press it yet. I'm gonna' burn it again."

"Too bad," said Scott. "You going to Belmar this weekend?" he asked Mason.

"Nope. Bay Head."

"Ooh, schmoozing with the upper crust, are we?"

"Not hardly. I'm the help. *Blue Cactus* strikes again."

"Strikes is the right word for it," said Scott.

"Get bent," said Mason playfully. "Come on, Mack. Let's go."

Mason hung his lab coat back on a hook and we headed for the door. He looked over his shoulder, "See ya', Scott."

"Aloha, Man."

"Nice to meet you," I said to Scott.

"Likewise," he said, but I didn't believe him.

Chapter Four

We left the lab and headed for Clinton. The countryside is really lush and green around Mason's house with horse farms and all kinds of historical landmarks. If you believed all the signs on the buildings you'd have to imagine that George Washington slept through the entire Revolutionary War. Who knows? Maybe he did. Billie met us with a couple of cold beers as soon as we drove up to the house. I could hear some *Dire Straits* in the background, and one of Billie's friends was swinging in a hammock stretched between two trees. "Hi ya', Brother," she had greeted me, "come meet my friend Gail."

She walked me over to the hammock and said, "Gail, this is my baby brother, Mack."

"He looks all grown up to me," said Gail. "Nice to meet you, Mack."

"Nice to meet you, too, Gail. You live around here?"

"Right down the road. I live right above Baker's Tavern. My folks own the place."

"That sounds handy," I said.

"In school, I was voted least likely to get a D.U.I."

"I'll bet," I laughed. "Are any of the band members here?"

"Just my husband, Peter. He's the keyboard player."

"I know Peter," I said. "I'm gonna' go inside and say hello. I'll see ya' later."

Gail kept on swinging in the hammock, and I took my beer inside to find Peter. I had met him once before when I went to one of their gigs about two years back. We talked about music and how they were looking for a percussionist, but living fourteen hundred miles away makes for a lousy commute. I couldn't take the job. Then they found Mitch. It's a good thing they did because he's a much better percussionist than I am. He's also a hell of a scientist from what I understand. I found Peter inside sitting at Mason's Steinway grand piano. I told him, "Good thing you don't have to lug that thing around, huh, Peter."

"Mack! When did you get here?"

"'Bout a minute ago. I met Gail outside. She's very pretty."

"Thanks. Man, it's good to see you."

"You, too. I can't wait to jam. I got a little rust though. Haven't even seen any of the set lists."

"Ridin' a bicycle, Man. You've played it all before except maybe the *Cold Play*. But they're not too bad. Just be glad we're not doing any *Dave Mathews*. Can you believe his drummer?" he asked.

"He's on Mars. They all are. The bass player is just as good. I'd give anything to play with a bottom like that."

"Don't let John hear you say that. He has a hard time accepting that there are bass players better than he is."

"He's not here, is he," I asked in a hushed tone.

"No, relax. He and Michael won't be here until five."

Michael was the other guitar player besides Mason. Most bands didn't need two lead guitar players, but then most bands didn't consist of four chemical engineers and a private investigator. Life is strange, and sometimes it's best to be strange right along with it.

Chapter Five

Michael and John showed up with Bill who I'd met earlier at the lab. They didn't waste any time getting into the beer. I'm sure it has something to do with loosening up before a band practice. *Right.* I was hitting them pretty hard, too - just finishing my fourth in less than two hours. But it felt good just to kick back for a while and look over the set lists with the rest of the band.

They were getting itchy and starting to fiddle around with the P.A. system and all the cords. Then there was the tuning. It's amazing how three guitar players can tune with electronic gizmos and still be out of tune. They sounded pretty close to me, but engineers can be kind of anal sometimes. They claimed that the guitars weren't "voiced" right. They would play in tune in one chord and then be out on another. The best thing is to just split the difference, but the compromise always seems to take about a half-hour.

Man, this brings me back, I thought. I then remembered one of the reasons I didn't like playing in a band. There were too many complications for the most part. But you can't really play the congas by yourself, so the best thing to do is just shut up and put up with it. *That's okay, guys, there's plenty of beer. I'll wait.*

We finally got around to playing and I was surprised to hear that they were a lot tighter than I remembered them. Some of it sounded pretty darned good for a bunch of old farts banging out classic rock in Hunterden County.

After a while some neighbors came rolling in and along with the wives and girlfriends of the band, we had a rather sizable audience. It was the most fun I'd had playing music in a very long time. I used to gig with a flutist in Melbourne, but he was a recovering alcoholic, so I couldn't drink. There's definitely a difference with a well-oiled group of musicians. I know it sounds pathetic to say that the music is better on booze, but let's just call it the sixth member of the band.

Chapter Six

Scott Palmer was the first person I saw when I arrived at the house in Bay Head on the night of the gig. I had borrowed an old VW Bug that Mike, the guitar player, was fixing up. I thought it was a really nice gesture, and I made a mental note to buy him a fender or something.

It was curious as to how Scott managed to get himself invited. He never would have known about the party if it weren't for Mason mentioning it to him at the lab. It was still another example of a gut feeling that I couldn't shake. I didn't like the guy no matter how hard I told myself that maybe I should give him a break. He looked past me at Peter's wife, Gail, as we walked up the drive. He pretended to be glad to see me, "Matt, you're late. There's a keg of Henninger with your name on it," he said.

"My name's not Henninger," I said. "It's *Mack*."

"Hey lighten up, Buddy. It's time to party," he said.

"I'm here to work, Scott. *Then* I get to drink, if I'm lucky."

"Yeah, whatever," he said. "Where's Mason?"

Ahh, there's the real question. Why is this guy following Mason around? I thought.

"I couldn't tell you. Try the patio. He should be setting up with Mike and John." He still had his eyes on Gail. She ignored him, and I got the distinct impression that she had been through this particular drill before. Gail was a sharp lady. I'd known the type when I worked as a homicide dick for about four years in Melbourne, Florida. I had a female partner once who could make a wise-guy nervous just by looking at him. Gail was about to lay into Scott when Peter came up behind her and slipped his arm around her waist, "How's my girl?" he asked.

"Thirsty," she said never taking her eyes off of Scott Palmer.

"Well, let me buy you a drink, Pretty Lady," said Peter.

"Sounds good to me," she said.

Scott pretended that I gave a shit what was on his mind when he asked me, "So Mack," *at least he got my name right,* "what are you guys gonna' play tonight?"

"I'm not sure," I lied. "I'll just look at the list a few minutes before we go on."

"You must be good," he said trying to shmooze me.

"I'm the best," I said. *So don't try to fuck with me,* I thought, but decided not to add to my growing dislike of the guy.

Chapter Seven

My sister Billie showed up with her eyes kind of dilated which seemed to piss me off, but hell, I guess I'm not my sister's keeper. I asked her, "Billie, you okay?"

"Of course, I'm okay. What's that supposed to mean?"

"Nothing. I was just wondering how you're doing, that's all."

"I'm *right there*, Mack. I just wish I could sit in tonight."

"You sound alright to me," I was referring to her damaged vocal chords.

"At this volume I'm strictly maple and honey, Honey, but you know Mason and John are gonna' play the turn 'em up game sooner or later. I gotta' save the pipes for the money projects, Sweetie, shitty as it is."

"I wish you could get points, Billie," I said, referring to the financial arrangement that pays performers for back-end sales rather than an up-front salary for studio work.

"I would have cleaned up on that Hadie Carlton CD, that washed-up bitch."

"Careful, Honey, your talons are showing."

"I'm kidding, Mackie. You *know* I really love Hadie."

"Save it, Billie. It's me, remember? You can hate anyone you want in front of me, but make sure it stops there."

"God, do I sound that bad? I was a headliner once, wasn't I, or was that just a dream?"

"You were *there*, Billie. You're *still there* for a lot of us."

"I love you, Mack."

"That's what brothers are for."

~

Scott Palmer was smoking a joint on the dune crossover to the beach when we took our first break. He motioned me over, "Dude, you want some of this?"

"No thanks," I said. I never was a grass head. I didn't have anything particular against it, though. I've done a lot of gigs with dudes that got high, and they always stayed with the program, but it always made me kind of paranoid. Sex was always kind of lame on a high, too. I guess I was born too late or something.

"Suit yourself," said Scott. "It's really good shit, though."

"I can tell." It smelled like a skunk.

"You seen Mason?" he asked. "I'm sure he'd like some of this."

That struck me as a little bit odd because I've never known Mason to be a pot-head. He likes his single malt scotch and cognac, but that's about it.

"I haven't seen him. He's probably on the beach with Billie."

"You mean Billie Willis?" he asked. "I used to love to hear her sing until she blew up in that marathon."

"What did you say?" I asked him.

"Billie Willis. I heard she sang at a marathon benefit for some kid's charity event. Six hours, they said. Now she ain't worth shit. But I guess we all make mistakes."

"She's my sister." *You asshole I should have added.*

"No shit," said Scott. "Hey, I didn't mean any disrespect."

"Forget it," I told him, but my eyes told him that *I* wouldn't. "We all make mistakes."

Chapter Eight

When I found Billie and Mason sitting on the beach, I snuck up behind them and said, "I'm glad to see you kids still have your clothes on."

"I can remember a time when we wouldn't," said Billie.

"Yeah, like last month in Barbados," said Mason laughing.

"That doesn't count," said Billie. "It's a foreign country."

"I saw your friend, Palmer, up at the house," I told them.

"He's no friend of mine, Mack. True, we drive to Belmar sometimes, but it's strictly a carpool as far as I'm concerned. He bothers me sometimes. I think I'm gonna' stop riding with him."

"What is it that bothers you about him except for the fact that he's a world class asshole?" I asked him.

"You noticed, huh? I don't like the company he keeps."

"You think he's selling out?" I asked.

"I think he would if he could. He asked me one time if I ever came across any notes on EMR concussion values. I know that's not anything we use for communication vehicles."

"What's an EMR concussion value," I asked naturally.

"Light pulses. It's how star wars technology knocks out enemy missiles. The light doesn't burn the nose cone. It bashes it with light."

"I've never heard of that," I told him.

"Haven't you ever read Clancey's, *The Cardinal of the Kremlin?*"

"Can't say that I have."

"Well, that's what it's about. Actually, that's how Reagan won the cold war. We beat the Russians with money," said Mason.

"What do you mean?" I asked him.

"We were spending about four percent of our GNP, our gross national product, on defense development, mostly star-wars. Russia had to spend about nineteen percent of hers just to match us. We bankrupted them trying to keep up with us.

We never really got star-wars off the ground, but we were determined to continue on until we did. Now the technology is evolving into something entirely different. I'm talking about EMR concussion pulses from space to the surface of the earth."

"You're not serious?" I demanded. I had never heard of anything so fantastic and blatantly *evil*.

"I wish I wasn't. I'm pretty sure that we have the technology to pinpoint a person here on earth and bash in his skull with a point of light in the form of an EMR concussion."

"Then why didn't we take out Saddam Hussein instead of going to war with Iraq?" I asked.

"If I told you, you wouldn't believe me."

"Try me," I said.

"Okay. Economics," he said seriously.

"You mean oil," I said.

"Oil is only part of it. We had an aging fleet of cruise missiles that we needed to use as well as a lot of other military toys that needed replacing for one reason or another. If it ain't broke, congress won't let you fix it."

"That's a pretty sick reason to go to war, Mason."

"Funny, I can't think of any really good ones."

"How did we get on this subject, anyway?" I asked him.

"You mentioned Scott. I think he'd sell his soul for thirty pieces of silver."

"You think he's selling developments from your lab to the government?"

"If he isn't already, it's only a matter of time. I can read him like a book. He fits the profile perfectly."

"What profile is that?"

"Corporate espionage. He's got no family that I know of, no girlfriend, no friends at the lab, except he tells everyone who'll listen that he and I are good pals just because we surf the same ocean occasionally."

"Why doesn't the government develop their own technology? Why steal it from others in the first place?"

"Because they can't draw the talent. A Captain in the Air Force makes about thirty thousand bucks a year, plus housing. The private sector attracts all the talent that actually moves the cutting edge. It's the same old story – money."

"Why is he so interested in what you're working on?" I asked him.

"Because if you could dope a big enough ruby rod, you could accelerate a pulse beyond light speed. Theoretically, you could excite a nuclear reaction from a ridiculous distance."

"You mean like from earth orbit?" I asked.

"Possibly. Could you imagine an enemy in space able to attack a target on the ground and be effectively invulnerable due to the vast distance from the battle it could maintain?"

"It makes star-wars look like a bow and arrow, Mason. What in the world makes people want to invent things like that?"

"What else? Power."

"The power to kill from an impossible distance. My, oh my, look how evolved we've become," I couldn't help remarking.

"Better us than them, Mack."

"What's to stop someone like Scott from selling it to the highest bidder?"

"Good point."

"So, what are you doing about it?" I asked.

"I'm goofing with him," said Mason.

"What does that mean?"

"I've been feeding him erroneous conclusions. He may be smart enough to steal, but he's not smart enough to know that he's stealing worthless information."

"You better not play around with him, Mason. If his friends find out what you're doing, you might find yourself being audited or something."

"I'm being very careful, Mack. If I'm right, the whole thing should blow up in his face very soon."

"I hope you know what you're doing," I said.

"I do, too, Mackie. I do, too."

Chapter Nine

W e made our way back to the party after a short while measured by a Corona with lime. The party guests were starting to get a little rowdy and we were anxious to turn way up and rattle a few door jams. Sometimes when the music gets loud enough, you can feel it in your stomach.

We usually don't get to play that loud in Hunterden, but in Bay Head, if it's before ten at night everybody keeps their mouths shut. One never knows whom one is complaining about. It wouldn't do to piss off a state senator just because he didn't invite you to his party. Besides, you could always crash it, and nobody would even notice. I was sure that was exactly what Scott did.

I was sure he wasn't invited. It was definitely the wrong mix of people for him. He seemed to stand out like a lumberjack at a tree hugger rally. All the engineers who made up the band were letting down their hair, but Scott seemed to try a little too hard. Two words that come to mind are *"forced,"* and *"unnatural."*

There was another guy at the party who didn't seem to fit in either, but I liked him. His whole makeup screamed harmless. He looked like an academic - complete with the nerd pocket protector. He wore tan slacks with a white shirt and a raspberry, cashmere sweater – the arms in a casual loop tied around his neck. I didn't notice his shoes on purpose. I knew they were docksiders just by looking at the rest of his outfit. Aside from being a walking cliché, his smile seemed genuine, and he kind of gave me a good feeling. I introduced myself during the next break after the second set. Extending a big paw, I said, "I'm Mack Willis."

"Yes, the bongo player," he said warmly and then added, "I'm enjoying your music. My name is Victor Reese," as he shook my hand.

"Pleased to meet you," I said. "You live here?" I asked him knowing it was extremely unlikely.

"No, no, heavens no. I'm from halfway around the globe. Or almost half way," he said. "I live on the big island of Hawaii. Wiamea is the name of the city. It's about a half-hour from the foot of Mauna Kea."

"I take it Mauna Kea is a mountain," I said. You can't put anything past a sharp P.I. like yours truly.

"That's right," he said. "A very high mountain. It's where a group of eleven large telescopes are perched nearly fourteen thousand feet above sea level."

"Sounds like you're an astronomer," I commented deftly.

"Very astute, Mr. Willis. I am, indeed."

"What brings you to New Jersey, Mr. Reese?"

"Actually, this party," he said rather cryptically. I got the impression that he didn't want to volunteer any further information that might tip off his true intentions. As usual I was wrong. He was just being purposely mysterious because when I commented that six thousand miles is a long way to travel to attend a party, he told me that he routinely deals with distances impossibly greater than that – as in the stars.

"Why this party?" I asked because I was sure he wanted me to.

"To meet your brother-in-law, Mason." *He knew who I was*

before I introduced myself.

"Is he expecting you?"

"I doubt it.   I only recently decided to make the trip and wanted to talk to him before he had the chance to turn me down."

"Sounds like an ambush," I said somewhat amused and intrigued.

"Of sorts. Do you intend to warn him?"

"On the contrary. Let me introduce you." I couldn't wait to hear what an astronomer from Hawaii traveled all the way to New Jersey to ask my slightly mad-scientist of a brother-in-law. "But I should warn you," I said, "he's kind of in a party mood - even though he's working. You might not want to talk shop at this moment unless you're also a musician."

"I'm afraid I'm not," he glanced at his docksiders. "A bit of a tin ear for the most part."

"But you said you like the music, right?" *Eternally fishing for a little encouragement. How shameless,* I scolded myself.

"Absolutely. *Cold Play* is one of my favorite bands. Do you play any *Dave Mathews?*"   He raised his eyebrows and had hope in his voice.

"Not this gig."

Chapter Ten

"**M**ason! Come meet a friend of mine," I said across the room maybe a little too loudly. I was feeling the beer just like everyone else. Mason walked over and told me we were going back up in about five minutes.

"Cool," I said. "Mason, I'd like you to meet Vick Reese. He's from Hawaii," I sounded just like Victor and I were old friends.

"Dr. *Victor* Reese," said Mason. "I've read some of your theoretical calculations. Your work is very far reaching, Doctor," he said.

"Please, call me Victor. Are you interested in astronomy, Mason? May I call you Mason?"

"By all means, Victor. Sure, I like astronomy. Who doesn't?"

"I should have known you'd be familiar with his work," I said. "Is there anything you don't read, Mason?"

"Music," he said laughing. "I play by ear."

"Figures," I said. "Can I get you guys a beer?"

"Sure," said Mason.

"None for me," said Victor. "I'm working."

As I went to get our beers I heard Mason ask him, "You're working? Tonight?"

"Yes, as a matter of fact I'm here to meet you, Mason."

"Uh oh, here it comes," he said.

"I'd like an interview if you could arrange some time for me - say perhaps an hour or so? Not tonight of course."

"Well, if someone comes all the way to New Jersey from Hawaii to talk to me for an hour or so what can I say. I'd be delighted to talk with you."

"I knew you'd say that. I'm familiar with some of your work as well."

"Naturally. That's why you're here. You want a better wire."

"Oh this is going much better than I had hoped," said Victor. "Do you think the application is possible?"

"Tomorrow, Victor. Grab yourself a beer and take a load off. I'll be glad to let you know where we are with the wire, but I'd like to clear it with Mike Becker. He's the co-inventor on this project. I trust you'll keep this strictly off the record until we go to product."

"Of course, of course!" said Victor smiling. "Yes, I think I will have that beer now, Mason. I feel like celebrating."

"Me too," said Mason, "Soon as I can find that conga player with my beer."

Chapter Eleven

O n my way to the keg, I saw Scott through one of the dining room windows. He was standing outside between the party house and the one next door. He seemed to be alone, and I wondered what the hell he was doing out there. I walked closer to the window frame and bent down to say something clever if it ever came to mind. I never got the chance. Scott was vomiting. He was violently sick with his chest heaving. I decided not to say anything clever or otherwise and to just get the hell out of there before he straightened up and happened to see me.

Imagine my surprise when after filling up a couple beer glasses for Mason and myself, I see Scott waiting in line for another beer. Man, that's dedication. I've heard of catching a buzz, but this guy is into world class abuse. The last thing I think I'd want after getting sick is another beer. Oh, well, to each his own. *What a screwball.* When he saw me he said, "Hey, Matt."

"It's Mack," I made no effort to hide my irritation. "M.A.C.K. It stands for Mackenzie. Mackenzie Willis, the conga virtuoso!"

"Yeah, Mack. I get it," he said, but I didn't believe it.

"How are you feeling, Scott?" I asked him - possibly to demonstrate the fact that I just saw him bent over decorating his shoes. I wasn't even sure of my own motivation where this guy was concerned. One minute I felt sorry for him, and the next I was back to an uneasy feeling that he's up to no good. I figured that the only thing I had going for me is that he was sure to underestimate me. He's an engineer. I'm just a simple P.I. who likes to play the congas when I'm not taking pictures of women cheating on their husbands, isn't that right? Well, that's just the way I wanted to play it for the time being anyway. Mason said he could handle this guy, but he'd been wrong before.

I got back to Mason with the beers just in time to go back on stage. The set was magical if nothing else. Mason was really reaching during the lead of *Crossroads,* and he got out cleanly on both breaks. I swear if I didn't know better I could have closed my eyes and sworn that *Eric Clapton* was on stage with us. I knew that he'd never played that purely before. When he made eye contact, I thought I saw him wink and shrug his shoulders as if to say, *hell, even I don't know where that came from.* Like I said, magical. I was in a trance also, playing just a little bit above my head. I was pulling off flams and rolls so tightly that I completely forgot about the volleyball injury that I sustained about three months back. It completely bent back my metacarpal tendon, which blew up like a balloon for about three days. I couldn't even shift gears in my little Porsche let alone play the congas.

Now, I was in a groove where I'd been once before when I played with Billie at the Filmore East. *Jesus, that seemed like a lifetime ago.* After *Crossroads*, we jumped right into *Strange Brew* by *Cream.* The harmonies were right on, and the crowd really seemed to be getting into it. Sticking to what was working, Mason then led us into *Sunshine of Your Love*, also by *Cream* and then finally, *Born Under a Bad Sign.* It was old British blues at its best. If we could have played that well on a regular basis, we all could have quit our day jobs. Not that Mason ever would. Science is a religion with Mason. He has a sense of responsibility to make us see what is right in front of our noses but usually goes unnoticed. Me, I could care less. When the oil runs out, we'll find alternative energy sources. We'll find the inventions when necessity is our mother or something like that. Or maybe it's that inventions are a mother of a necessity.

In either case, the beer was going down great and so was the gig. I hadn't felt so "in place" in a long time. That's when the bombshell landed. She was blond and beautiful and not at all shy. She had the kind of legs that went all the way up if you know what I mean. She was a very fancy dresser, but she was also a little drunk. After leaning on me for a little while, she asked if I'd walk her to her car. Gentleman that I am, I first checked out her butt and then said, "Absolutely."

We got to her car, which was a fairly new Jag, (I really don't care for the new ones), with a ragtop and some pretty nice smelling leather to tell you the truth. She wanted to play kissy face with me for a while to sober up before making the trip home. I couldn't blame her. I'm a hell of a lot more fun than a cup of hot coffee. When I asked what her name was, she threw me for a loop by saying, "It's classified."

"That's a strange name," I said. "Classified what? Classified Zeta Jones?"

"I'd tell you, but then I'd have to kill you," she said with a giggle.

"Why don't you kiss me instead," I said. "I don't really care about your name anyway."

"It's Martie Coleman," she said.

"Kiss me, Martie," I said. "I need to sober up too, and I think you're just the ticket."

"Want to drive me home?" she asked.

"Can't," I said. "I'm working."

"Hey, you're in the band, aren't you?" she asked.

"Guilty as charged," said I. "Did you like the music?"

"It was okay, I guess. Will I see you again?" she asked.

"Give me your phone number, and it's a sure bet," I said.

"You talk like Humphrey Bogart, Mack."

"So you know my name," I said somewhat confused because I didn't remember giving it to her.

"Back at the party, I heard the guitar player call you Mack."

"Oh, well, that explains it," I said, but I didn't believe it. I wasn't talking to anyone when she dropped her bomb. *That seems very interesting,* said the little voice inside of my head.

"Here's my number," she said as she handed me her card. "Call me."

"I will," I said glancing at the card. "The very next time I find myself in need of The Department of Defense."

"I'm just a secretary, Mack. I was only kidding about being classified," she said just a little too much like the dumb blond that she wasn't. As it all started to come clear to me, I realized that there was something else that she wasn't. She wasn't really drunk. She was very lucid, but for some reason wanted to appear drunk. I can tell the difference. All those years of painstaking field research in bars finally paid off after all. You see, I've been around the block a few times and even paid attention once or twice, believe it or not. After Martie Coleman (if that's really her name) drove off, I was left with an all too familiar feeling. I had the distinct impression that I'd just had my pocket picked. Oh, I knew I still had my wallet, but that's not what she was after.

She knew I'd call her, so she could pull a few more of my strings. She'd peaked my interest with considerably more than her bust-line. I never could resist a mystery and this lady was spelled with a capital M. I'd call her all right and then just hang on for the ride. A pretty nice ride at that, and of course, I had to find out just what she wanted from Mason.

Chapter Twelve

When it came time to pack up and leave the party, Scott was talking to Victor Reese in the parking lot. *Man, that guy gets around*, I thought to myself. But that wasn't the half of it. His next little encounter was deeply rooted in spooksville. To this day I'm not sure that I heard the exchange correctly, but I'll try my best to relate it the way I thought it came across. After he left Victor, Scott returned to the party and headed straight for the bathroom. As luck would have it I felt the call of nature just at the right time to catch him talking to a rather strange looking fellow as they stood in the hallway outside the bathroom. As I approached, I was able to backtrack quickly before either man saw me and still stand close enough, (I thought), to catch their conversation. It went something like this: ". . . st because the cold war has ended, it doesn't mean that your obligation to your country has also ended."

"Keep your voice down, Dimitri. Someone might hear you."

"You are the one who needs to hear what I have to say. It is always the same with you."

"I am completing my assignment at the only pace that is reasonable."

"You seem to enjoy a lifestyle that is beyond the reach of your countrymen, and yet it is at their expense, *Scott*."

"You say my name as though it's a curse word."

"In some circles it is, but they use the name Uri. They feel that they are cursed with the inefficiency of a man named Uri - a man who expends the resources of his countrymen on *surfing lessons.*"

"I need access to my target, Dimitri. You know that."

"I know there is talk of bringing you home soon, Uri."

"The time will come when I'll return home a hero."

"It had better be a short time, Uri. A *very* short time."

Well, I don't have to tell you what that little gem brought to light. I was sure that Mason had no idea who or what he was dealing with. Scott's friends were the *real* bad guys. Most people were content to believe that with the fall of the Iron Curtain came the fall of international black ops; that the KGB simply went off into the countryside to become farmers or make vodka.

I was recently on a case in south Florida, which revealed an altogether different reality. I had come to learn that the actual number of KGB operatives has actually increased since the end of the so-called cold war. I had just discovered one of them named Uri, who is known as Scott Palmer and being worked by a control named Dimitri. The world just seems to get smaller and smaller. Now Martie Coleman's appearance was starting to make sense. I knew that if she was really just a secretary, I was really Captain Kangaroo. I backtracked to the parking lot in search of Mr. Greenjeans.

Chapter Thirteen

Mason was standing with Billie by the open driver's door of their Beamer. *A Beamer and a Lexus, I noted. Was Mason selling out? I know Billie went through all her money the year after she stopped touring.* I noticed that he had her face in his hands and was bending down trying to coax her into eye contact. *What's up with that?* I wondered. Then I could see that she was crying. I knew instantly what was bothering her. Every gig it's the same old same old. She wants to sing.

I knew that Mason offered her a couple of tunes in the third set as long as she stuck to Joni Mitchell or Carol King. I also knew that she would turn him down. Billie's much too animated for her own good. If she couldn't do her own stuff, which kills her vocal chords, then she always wants to do something like *Joplin's* rendition of *Bobby McGee* or *Slick's White Rabbit* from *Jefferson Starship*.

Mason's smart to turn her down. If her nodes come back in a big way, she won't get to work at all. That would break her heart for sure. I felt kind of bad for her as usual, but I didn't want to walk up to them when they were like that. What could I say? They both know that I know the score, so there's nothing *to* say. Things have a way of working themselves out. Maybe Mike can work the bugs out of that gizmo he promised her last year. He says it's just a matter of time, but that's the universal mantra of all engineers, I guess.

Mike says that he can compress her voice with a spinning speaker driven by a simple vocoder. Typically a vocoder is used for special effects or to change the quality of a voice, but Billie would never go for that. She doesn't even like a digital delay. She plays it strictly clean. But Mike's idea would only boost her volume controlled by a foot pedal. Since the whole thing is digital, there wouldn't be any increase in (hiss) or white noise. Pure EMR waves he liked to say. It sounds good on paper, but in reality he gets a lot of feedback.

When Mason got into the driver's seat, Billie walked around the car to the passenger's side. I got her attention and raised a finger as I trotted closer to their car. When she stopped to hear me, I asked, "You guys going to breakfast or straight home?"

"Just home, Mackie. I'm really tired tonight."

"I'll be home a little later," I told her. "I want to stop for one at Baker's Tavern."

"Watch your rearview mirror little brother," she said.

"What for, wolf packs?" I asked referring to the roadblocks that check for DUI's in Florida.

"No wolf packs, but the troopers can get pretty bored in Hunterden County."

"I got ya'. Don't worry. I'll be fine."

I watched them drive away and then made my way over to Mike's VW. As I reached over to place the key into the door-lock, I noticed the lock button was up. *That's strange. Maybe I just forgot to lock the car. After all, it's a pretty nice neighborhood so why be so paranoid? Because I always lock the door.*

My mind started racing. *Who* broke into my car? *Why* would someone break into my car? *What* was missing? The congas were in the trunk, but no one would steal . . . *Oh, hell,* I thought as I opened the door and tripped the latch for the front hood. The congas were still there. I looked around a little bit self-conscious of my actions, but it never hurts to be cautious. I half expected to see Joey Berio lurking around in the shadows. Maybe I was just being paranoid. I didn't keep anything valuable in the car - I just always lock up out of habit. I've never heard of an investigator who doesn't.

I knew it was that creep Palmer that had me jumpy. What the hell was he up to? What did his country hope to gain from him? Technology? They could steal that soon enough. No, something didn't add up. I wouldn't put it past Martie Coleman to try a little corporate espionage, but this Uri Palmer crap just didn't add up. What were they after if not Mason's wire technology? Why would Palmer return home a hero? Mason might not realize the danger of dealing with these characters. At that moment I was very glad that I decided to take the job with Blue Cactus. I thought that Mason might need a watchdog whether he knew it or not.

Chapter Fourteen

When I got to Baker's Tavern, I saw Peter and Gail just about to enter the front door. When they saw me pull in, they waited for me to park the Bug and catch up to them.

"Cool party, huh Mack?" asked Peter.

"Way cool, as they say. You sounded good tonight, Peter. I like the new keyboard."

"So do I."

"So Gail tells me you guys live up there," I motioned to the exterior stairs leading to their apartment.

"That we do," said Peter. "Gail grew up in the house at the end of the drive."

"Then when I was in high school," continued Gail, "my folks let me live in the apartment with my older sister."

"Sounds cool," I said. "I'll bet you had a lot of parties."

"Not really. We were both like a couple a nerds. You know, National Honor Society and all that."

"It kinda' runs in the family," said Peter.

"I'll bet." I had the feeling that you could subtract my I.Q. from theirs and still end up with a hell of a nice bowling score. "Let me buy you guys a drink," I offered.

"No way," said Gail. "These are on me. Remember I get a family discount."

"Must be nice."

When we entered the tavern, I could see a few college kids playing darts and working on a pitcher of beer. There were the usual old crows sitting at the bar, sprinkling salt in their glasses and furiously trying their luck at the scratch-off tickets they sold next to the register. One of them looked up and said, "Uh oh, there goes the neighborhood," as he motioned to us just entering the room. Another one said, "Gail honey. Come over here and give your old uncle a kiss." He had apparently decided to drink his dinner.

"You're not my uncle, Mr. Bailey," she laughed like it was a long running joke between them.

"Well, you can't blame a guy for trying," said Bailey. "Peter, who's your friend?"

"This is Mack Willis, Billie's brother. He's visiting from Florida."

"Pleased to meet you, Mack" said Bailey almost falling off of his stool. "You an engineer?"

"No, I'm afraid not," I said.

"Glad to hear it," said Bailey, which produced a hearty laugh around the bar. "What brings you to cold country, Mack?"

"Music," I told him. "Mason asked me to sit in with the band."

"What do you play," he asked.

"Conga drums."

"You got any black blood in ya'?" he raised an eyebrow.

"Not that I know of," I told him.

"Too bad."

This brought more laughter from the regulars seated around the bar. The room had a good feeling to it, and I got the distinct impression that I could fit in really well in Hunterden County, not that I could ever take the cold winters. We ordered boilermakers which consisted of thirteen ounces, (a Baker's dozen), of Bass ale which we used to wash down shots of peppermint schnapps. The combination was really refreshing, sort of like the red and white after dinner mints that you get in a restaurant. After the second round, Gail excused herself to go to the bathroom, which gave me the chance to ask Peter if he knew Martie Coleman.

"Nope. Never met her. Why do you ask?"

"She was at the party."

"She nice?"

"She's very pretty, but that's not the point."

"So, what *is* the point?" asked Peter.

"Well, she sort of came on to me, I guess."

"You guess? I'll bet you make a hell of a living as a P.I., Mack."

"Wait a minute, wise ass, let me explain. She asked me to walk her to her car like she was too drunk to make it on her own. Then one thing leads to another, and we start kissing in the front seat of her car."

"What kind of car?" he asked.

"What difference does it make?" I thought Peter was making fun of me.

"I'm just trying to get the picture," said Peter. "So you're sitting in the front seat of her. . ."

"Jaguar," I offered.

"Jaguar," continued Peter, "and what happened then?"

"Not much, she just gave me her card and asked me to call her."

"That's it?" he asked.

"Just about, except that she wasn't drunk," I told him.

"What makes you so sure."

"I don't know. It's just a feeling I got. Like she was play acting or something."

"Maybe she just wanted to meet you."

"That's what I thought," I told him, "until I read her business card. She works for The Department of Defense."

"In Washington?"

"No, New York City. Her office is in The Federal Building across from the World Financial Center. So what do you think?"

"I don't know," he said with mock seriousness. "I've never kissed in the front seat of a Jaguar."

Now I knew Peter was making fun of me, "Very funny. And here I thought all engineers were dull."

"Ouch."

"No, really. Do you think there's any connection to this woman and Mason's work?"

"I don't see how," he said. "The government would approach Bell Labs directly and inform them that they wish to purchase their product."

"So what happens if the product is not actually for sale yet?" I asked hypothetically.

"Then I can't imagine how they would even know about it. I'm not even sure that I know about it, and I work at the damned place. What exactly are you talking about, Mack?"

"Oh, I don't know. I'm just a little worried about Mason, that's all."

"Mason can take care of himself," said Peter.

"Yeah, I suppose you're right. So what do you think I should do about Martie Coleman?"

"You said she's pretty, right?"

"Yeah, so?"

"And she asked you to call her?"

"That's right."

"Well, I know what *I'd* do."

Chapter Fifteen

I got home to Mason and Billie's house at about 1:40 A.M. They were still up - despite Billie's claim that she was so tired. When I walked up to the front patio where they were talking, I noticed them stop almost in mid-sentence. *What's up with that?* I wondered. I've never been particularly nosey where Billie is concerned, but I never thought she kept any secrets from me either.

"Hi guys," I said trying to be casual about catching them not talking around me.

"Hey, Mackie," said Billie.

"Hi, Mack," said Mason. "How was Baker's Tavern?"

"I had fun. Peter and Gail showed up, and we drank boiler makers."

"Drink some water before you go to bed, Mackie. Otherwise, you'll get really dehydrated and have a headache in the morning."

"Believe it or not it's not my first time, Billie."

"And did you have a headache in the morning?" she asked.

"Good point."

"Mason, I'm going to bed," she said standing up and kissing him on the top of his head. "Let the kitties in if you hear them. Night, Mack."

"Night, Billie."

"Good night, Billie. I'll be up in a little while," Mason told her.

We watched her go through the front door and close it behind her. I asked Mason, "Is everything all right?"

"Everything's *never* all right with your sister, Mack."

"What's that supposed to mean?"

"Nothing really. It's just that everyone has their problems, that's all."

"But that's not what you said. You said with *my* sister."

"You know she's depressed about her voice and all."

"So why doesn't she just do something else?" I suggested. "She could play an instrument if it has to be music."

"She thinks she's too old for that."

"Oh nonsense" I told him. "She's certainly not too old to play a tambourine."

"She'd feel like a bimbo. She thinks only stage bimbos play tambourines."

"Remember the song called *We Can Work It Out* by the Beatles? Do you suppose Ringo Starr thought of himself as a stage bimbo?"

"Tell *her*, Mack. Don't tell me. I like percussion instruments. You *know* that. I'm sure she could handle a rusty knife and a washboard like they do in Junkanoo music. But if she isn't singing, she isn't the star."

"I guess it takes a certain mindset to be an accompanist."

"A musicianship if nothing else. I'm just glad she never learned the guitar. You know she'd play too loud," he said laughing.

I laughed too and then changed the subject. "So what's the deal with Palmer?"

"You mean, Uri," he said deadpan.

"You know about him?"

"And Dimitri," he said. "It's a cinch if you know his name is

Uri, then you know about Dimitri, even if you don't know him by name."

"I heard him talking to Scott, who called him Dimitri. What's their story, Mason?"

"Can you *believe* those guys?" he asked with a chuckle. "They're such boners."

"Boners?" I asked confused.

"I guess I mean boneheads, Mack. They're a big joke around the lab."

"Dimitri works for Bell Labs too?"

"No, but he shows up at all the social functions, like we're not going to notice him sticking out like a sore thumb. We call them Boris and Natasha when they're not around."

"And they don't know that you're on to them?"

"I think Scott knows or rather *Uri*. But Dimitri's a real dolt. All he does is visit the porn clubs and push Uri around now and then. Everybody's on to them, so they're harmless. Actually they're sort of useful. We've been asked to kind of string them along for a while."

"What do you mean string them along?" I asked still not getting the gist of it.

"Remember the work I showed you in the lab?"

"Yeah. That's some fascinating stuff."

"It is fascinating, Mack, but that room is all a fake."

"You're kidding?"

"No way, man. I might be able to mix up a little chicken soup and then heat it up on a Bunsen burner, but that's about all. The real work is in an entirely different building. Uri isn't allowed in there."

"I should have known you had this under control," I said.

"It's still a tricky business. I have to act like it's the real thing or some people might get hurt."

"What do you mean?" I asked - brick that I am. I was sure that ten thousand of me and a little mortar could build a very nice schoolhouse.

"It's not the technology per se' that they're after. It's a name."

"Someone on our side I take it."

"You guessed it, Buddy. Someone they think is on their side and works in their research and development complex."

"How do they hope to discover this mole?"

"Uri, naturally."

"And, of course, it will be the wrong name."

"Right again, my conga playing friend."

"But you said that Uri knows that you're onto him."

"That's right, but he's playing both sides against the middle. He plans to sell the process to the U.S. Government as well as the Russians."

"But he must know that he can't get away with that. They'll fry him."

"He might be able to run for a while. He's dying anyway, so if he can get a few months of fun, what's the harm?"

"Somehow I don't think the bad guys will see it that way."

"Which bad guys are they?" asked Mason.

"Take your pick."

"Well, I guess it goes with the territory."

"There's something else I think you should know," I told him.

"Martie Coleman," he said with a twinkle in his eye. "I could tell she liked you."

"You know Martie Coleman. Why doesn't that surprise me? She's the Martie that the woman at the station referred to, isn't she?"

"She's a gem. The whole fake lab idea was hers."

"She asked me to call her. I figured she was trying to get to you," I told him.

"No, Mack. She's trying to get to you."

"Is there anything else I should know? Like maybe the C.I.A. are masquerading as your garbage men?"

"Every Thursday," he said.

"I'm serious, Mason. Who else figures into this equation that I don't know about?"

"I'd tell you, but then I'd have to kill you," said the asshole that he is sometimes.

"Never mind," I said.

"Okay, okay. Bill," he said simply.

"Bill? You mean the security guard, slash band manager, Bill?" I asked feeling just a little bit left out of the loop.

"He's N.S.A."

"Naturally."

Chapter Sixteen

I called Martie Coleman's office the next day and she agreed to join me for a drink after work. We met at the restaurant bar inside the World Financial Center across from Ground Zero. The drinks were strong, but the sushi plate we shared could have had a little more crabmeat, and the wasabi was about four hours old. I like it hot and fresh, just like my women. I'm sorry. I just couldn't resist that line. Martie Coleman just sort of brought out the beast in me.

She was dressed in a white satin skirt with a black patent leather belt and a scarlet blouse that caressed her curves in all the right places. She looked a lot more appetizing than the bonsai roll in front of us. Her open toe sandals spoke of a casualness that belied the typical atmosphere of the Federal Building where she worked, but I got the distinct impression that no one complained very much. She simply oozed a sexuality that was somewhat unsettling for the average under-active P.I. / conga player looking for any semblance of a smooth move. I decided to take a chance on honesty, "You're a remarkably pretty woman, Martie."

"Why, thank you, Mr. Willis. And I have to say you're rather handsome yourself."

"I'm glad you think so. I like to keep in shape." The truth of the matter was I control my weight by skipping meals and usually avoid any physical activity more strenuous than drinking beer in a golf cart.

"I'm glad you called me," she said.

"I could never resist a mystery. Curse of being a P.I."

"I'm no mystery, Mack. When I want something, I go after it, that's all."

"You kind of threw me for a loop the other night." I wanted her to think she had the upper hand - *alright* - *I guess she kinda' did.*

"The feeling's mutual," she said. "I was disappointed to end up riding home alone after our encounter."

"No significant other?" I asked her pointedly.

"I'm afraid not," she said. "I work rather a hectic schedule, and I'm expected to travel a lot."

"Ahh, the perils of being a spy, no doubt."

"I'm hardly a spy," she said. "Although, I'm not really a secretary like I told you before."

"I never believed it for a second. I knew it would have been a horrible waste of talent."

"What do you mean by that?" she asked, and then added, "Although, I like the sentiment."

"Well, you're obviously intelligent *and beautiful*, so if you were a secretary, it would only be a matter of time before you ascended to a higher position."

"Oh, I like a lot of different positions." she smiled and raised one eyebrow.

I couldn't believe this woman. I looked around me briefly for effect and then said, "Maybe there's a fire hose around here somewhere that I could use to put you out."

"I just have a healthy appetite, that's all."

"Yeah, well, try the sushi," I said fanning myself with the menu.

"Take the ferry with me, Mack."

"I took the train into Penn Station."

"Come. Take the ferry," she insisted.

"But how will I get home to Clinton?"

"I'll drive you home later – after you come with me."

"Where to," I asked.

"My car. It's in Hoboken in a parking garage. That's how I get to work. I don't live in the city."

"Where *do* you live?" I asked her.

"Sandy Hook. I inherited a beach house from my folks."

"You mean like that house the other night in Bay Head?" I asked her.

"No, nothing like that. That place was huge. My house is only about a third of the size of that one. It only has three bedrooms and one bath, but there's a nice little apartment over the garage. I think the beach is much nicer where I live, but then again, I'm prejudiced because I grew up there."

"It sounds nice," I told her.

"Come with me. Let me show it to you, and I'll cook for you."

"All that beauty *and* talent? You really can cook?"

"I have a lot of talents, Mr. Willis. I'd like to show them *all* to you if you'll let me," she said in a smoky sultry voice.

"You're incredible," I said truthfully.

"You don't know how right you are, but you will." She held up her hand to motion the waitress over, "Check please."

Chapter Seventeen

We got to Sandy Hook, New Jersey, about 7:45 in the evening. Martie whipped up a Caesar salad and some shrimp scampi in about twenty-five minutes. It was delicious. So was she. We sat on her couch by the fire and just wrapped ourselves up in each other's arms for a short while. It was a very nice feeling to connect with a beautiful woman. It had been some time for me, and I got the distinct impression that she had been alone for a while as well.

At about 10:00, we took a couple beers down to the beach for a walk. The surf was pounding right on shore because the tide was in. We had to walk up close to the dunes to stay out of the water. Our progress was a bit labored and slow, so she finally said, "Let's just sit here for a minute, okay, Mack?"

"Sounds good," I said.

"We should have brought a blanket," she said.

"Naw," I told her. "Blankets are for sissies. Back in Florida, blankets aren't allowed, just beer," I kidded her.

"Don't you get sand in your private places?" she asked.

"Yeah, but it's warm enough to swim in the ocean most of the time."

"Just you and the sharks, huh?" she asked.

"That's right. They know better than to mess with me." I decided to change the subject, "Tell me about Uri."

"I see you've been talking to Mason."

"I found out about Uri all by myself, Martie."

"That was quick. I understand you only arrived here in New Jersey three days ago," she said.

"Well, he's not very discreet, as I'm sure you know."

"You've noticed, huh?" she chuckled and took a long pull on her bottle of beer.

"The fake lab idea was pretty sharp on your part," I said.

"You didn't find that out by yourself. You may be a good P.I., but I doubt that you're a scientist also."

"Mason told me about it."

"I see," she said. "What else has he told you?" she asked with concern in her voice.

"Not much. Just that you intend to send a red herring to Russia in the way of a wrong name. I think it's cool."

"Well, I'm glad you think it's cool, but I'm kind of miffed at Mason for opening his big mouth."

"What's the matter, Martie? It's no big deal."

"Yes it is, Mack. It's a very big deal. A man's life is at stake."

"Well, you know I'm not going to tell anyone about it."

"That's not the point," she said. "This is a very delicate situation that has to be handled with kid gloves. Jesus, I can't believe that Mason is so careless sometimes."

"Take it easy, Martie."

"Would you take it easy if you held someone else's life in the balance? I didn't like this assignment in the first place. Now, I like it even less."

"Well, you got to meet me," I said with false braggadocio.

"I'm very glad I got to meet you, Mack, but you have to stay way out of all this. Leave the spy crap to the professionals."

"I thought you said you weren't a spy."

"Drop it, Mack."

"I'm not about to compromise your. . ."

"Look, Mack. I'm not going to discuss it with you. My work has to *stay* at work."

"Okay, okay," I said. "Let's change the subject."

"Good idea. I took you home to *forget* about work. Now where were we?"

"We were talking about getting sand in private places," I said.

"I've got a better idea. Let's go back to the house."

We walked slowly back to Martie's house, and I got the impression that she was really starting to warm up to me. It's always a magical moment for me when I first become intimate with a woman. For a moment it seemed like we were heading in that direction when we returned to the cozy sofa by the fire. Then the moment was suddenly turned off as abruptly as the flick of a switch.

I held Martie's head in my hands – wanting to find the warmth that I had found in her eyes – and saw that they were full of tears. The sight was like an icy hand wrapped around my heart. I felt a protective instinct well up inside of me and asked, "Martie, what's wrong?" She didn't answer me. "What?" I insisted. "Did I step on your feelings or something? My emotions can be kind of clumsy sometimes."

"Shhh," she closed her eyes.

"Are you okay?"

"Shhh."

I figured that I wasn't going to get an answer out of her any time soon, so I just held her head in my lap and stroked her soft blond hair. We stayed like that for what seemed to be a very long time. She just needed contact with another human, was all that I could figure. I was glad to oblige.

Sleep was pulling at my eyes around eleven, so I asked her, "You mind if I lay down for a while?" I didn't have a car, and I was pretty sure that Martie didn't feel like driving me home just then. I wanted to help her feel better, but there was nothing I could do. For some reason she just wasn't ready to share what was hurting her.

She asked me, "Is it okay if I drive you home in the morning?"

"I could take a bus." I knew the turnaround time to Clinton was about three hours.

"I want to drive you, Mack. I just have to close my eyes for a little while."

"Sure, I understand. Give me a blanket and I'll just crash here on the couch."

"I have a guest room, Mack."

"I like it here by the fire," I said.

She kissed me lightly on the lips and said, "Thanks."

"Thank *you*. Dinner was great and so was the company," I told her truthfully. She wasn't crying anymore, but I could see that her eyes were still red. I imagined that it might take her a little while to actually fall asleep. I, on the other hand, was soon out like a light.

Chapter Eighteen

Being the world class P.I. that I am, I soon discovered what was bothering Martie. When I woke up about six hours later, staring me right in the face was a photograph of the woman who was killed at the Clinton Train Station. She was the one with the lazy eye – killed by an ice dart, whatever the hell that is. I assumed that Martie knew the woman, but now I could see by the photograph that they were close.

Martie didn't have to say anything. I knew what was on her mind. She was kicking herself for becoming close to someone at work. For most people that would never be a consideration; however, in Martie's line of work she should know better. I wanted to talk to her about it, but I didn't think I should bring it up. Mason told me to forget about it, and I knew it would just upset her again.

We arrived back at Billie and Mason's about 10:00 A.M. the next day. Martie didn't stay for breakfast so all I fixed was some toast and coffee. I figured that Mason had already gone to work, and Billie wasn't up yet. It must have been a late one for her, or else she couldn't sleep. I worry about her sometimes because she takes pills to sleep and keeps them by her bedside. I told her that's a dangerous habit, but she doesn't listen to me most of the time.

I went up to her room and peeked in. She was still breathing. I felt stupid for my worries. *Of course,* she was still breathing. I went back downstairs and cleaned up some dishes that were left from the night before. Mike Becker, the other guitar player for Blue Cactus, stopped in, and I offered him a cup of coffee. He accepted, and we talked about the gig in Bay Head.

Mike was a pretty good player. He was better than the rest of the band to be totally honest. He had a real chance to be a full-time musician. All he needed was the desire. It was kind of sad because we both knew it would never happen. He would continue to work as an engineer at Bell Labs because he expended so much effort to get there. It was clearly the wrong reason to cling to a job.

Mason's case was different. He was invited on board right out of college because some of his teachers were retired Bell Labs engineers who could see his potential. All Mason had to do was say *"yes,"* but Mike had to say *"please."*

About twenty minutes later, Mason walked in with Victor Reese. He hadn't gone to work after all. The winding roads in Hunterden County are kind of confusing sometimes, so Mason had driven down the hill to the post office to show Victor the way up. They were going to have their meeting about the possible application of Mason's discovery. Mike was currently working with Mason on the real project that was kept hidden from Uri, so he was invited to stay and listen. I got to be a fly on the wall.

Mason began, "Hawaii's a long way from here, Victor. Didn't you ever consider e-mailing me?" he asked with humor in his voice.

"Oh, I needed to get away anyway. I'm afraid I had a little *island fever*, if you will."

"You get tired of Hawaii?"

"Not exactly. The work is fascinating, but it's a very remote location. It seems like only a representation of the civilized world."

"What do you mean?" asked Mason.

"Well, although we have all the comforts of home, the rest of the amenities are quite limited. The town I live in has a movie theater, but only one; there aren't many restaurants, and the cultural events are centered around the high school auditorium. We're not exactly going to get *The Phantom of the Opera*, if you know what I mean."

"But it must be a beautiful place. It sounds very exotic," said Mike.

"Oh, it's very nice. It has palm trees and tropical fruits and vegetables, but it rains a lot and we're not very close to the ocean," said Victor.

"What? No ocean?" questioned Mason.

"Not in Wiamea," said Victor.

"What about Wiamea Bay?"

"That's a different island. There are many different Wiameas. It means wide water so naturally there are a lot of them. My Wiamea is a small town where a lot of the scientific community lives. It's also the collection point for a lot of the data from the summit. The summit is called Mauna Kea where eleven large telescopes are positioned at about fourteen thousand feet. Wiamea receives the data and batches it to send to our sister locations in Australia and South

America. Our information from the cosmos is really a patchwork of photons collected from various positions around the Earth."

"So what do you hope to gain from my work?" asked Mason. "Why are you looking into a better wire?"

"Well, it's all about signal loss, isn't it? So I suppose the operative word here is photon. The patchwork of photons I spoke of is simply that - *photons*. That is the smallest unit of light that we are able to receive from the cosmos. As I'm sure you know, most of everything - everywhere is made up of dark matter.

Obviously, we call it dark matter because we receive less than a photon of radiation from those areas. Therefore, we assume that nothing is there. At least some of us make that assumption. But what if we were able to detect say, half a photon? I believe that we might perceive the universe in a completely new light so to speak."

"And if my wire does what I hope it will, the half-photon will be boosted to a value that is measurable on the collection grid of a hard drive, is that it?"

"Precisely," said Victor.

"What if the atmosphere blocks the signal from the reflective surface of the telescope?" asked Mason.

"That's the beauty of the summit," said Victor excitedly. The telescopes are above ninety-eight percent of the earth's atmosphere."

"It sounds cold," said Mason.

"About thirty-two degrees at sunset," said Victor.

"I haven't had much success yet, Victor," said Mason.

"But you will, I'm sure of it," he said excitedly.

"I can't promise any kind of length, you know," said Mason. "We could do maybe fifty feet in a vacuum, but you would need zero gravity for any kind of continuous roll-out."

"Fifty feet is more than enough. I plan to place a hard drive interface right at the base of the telescope. If I get any EMR evidence from a region of dark matter, then we'll get our zero G manufacturing module. I'm sure I can convince NASA that it's in all our interests to explore the dark matter with a signal boost. Do you really expect to accelerate a light impulse?" asked Victor.

"I hope so," said Mason. "It works out on paper, anyway."

"This puts a new twist on the concept of *the ether*, doesn't it? I mean, if light can be accelerated, the vehicle can't be a constant, isn't that true?"

"We're rewriting the science books on a regular basis now, Victor. How many moons does Jupiter have this week?"

"I get your point. When I get my wire, I'm sure we'll be writing a whole new chapter."

"If I can get fifty feet out of the lab, how do you expect delivery? It's not something I feel good about sending to Hawaii by UPS."

"I intend to wait for it. I'll put it in my luggage on the plane."

"What if I was months away?" asked Mason cryptically.

"I know you're close. Anyway it's worth waiting for. I don't mean to sound pushy, Mason, but, could you give me any kind of time frame?"

Mason looked over to Mike and waited for eye contact. He smiled slightly and said, "What do you think, Mike?"

Mike didn't say anything, but I perceived a slight hint of a nod and a smile. Mason then said, "We're close all right, Victor. Stop by the lab tomorrow, and you'll get your wire."

Actually, I followed about ninety percent of their egghead conversation pretty well. I figured that, all things considered, that made me a pretty smart fly.

"Outstanding!" said Victor. "I promise you, you won't be sorry. And, of course, it goes without saying that all of this will remain strictly between your office and mine."

"Uh, I think I've got a better idea, Victor. How about it remains between you and me?"

"All right, if that's the way you want it," said Victor.

"There's one other thing," said Mason.

"What's that?" asked Victor.

"I need you to destroy the wire."

"Excuse me?" queried Victor.

"After your test, whether or not you get a successful signal from dark matter, I need you to destroy the wire. You'll still have your data to take to congress or NASA."

"All right. How exactly would you like me to destroy it?" asked Victor.

"I'm glad you asked me that, Victor. There's an active volcano on your island on the southeast shore. In fact, it's the most intense continuous eruption in the world right now. I'm sure you're aware of it," said Mason.

"Of course," said Victor. Then he realized where Mason was going and he said, "You want me to place the wire before a lava floe."

"You got it. You'll get plenty more when the lab registers the patents and goes into production. You might even get an improved product if you can convince NASA for some space aboard the ISS. Who knows? You might end up with a celestial party-line," said

Mason in jest.

"Now, wouldn't that really be something," said Victor.

Chapter Nineteen

B illie came down a short time later and headed straight for the coffeepot. She wouldn't talk to anyone after she slept for any length of time until she had at least one cup. Mason thought he'd have a little fun at her expense. "Billie, the house is on fire."

No response.

"Billie, I'm moving to New Zealand."

No response.

"Billie, I'm having an affair."

No Response.

Finally she joined the group and said, "Put out the fire, don't forget to write, and you better treat her better than you treated me."

We all got a good laugh out of that. That's typical Billie; smart as a whip even when she's only half-awake. Mason introduced her to Victor, and she invited him to stay for dinner. She didn't have to include Mike because he always made himself at home and knew he was welcome. As it turned out, Mike had a date for dinner, but he hung around for lunch.

Victor took off to visit his mother in Seaside Heights, but said he'd try to make it back for dinner. Mason and Mike asked me to teach them some of the original tunes I wrote over the summer. A couple of R & B numbers seemed like they could work out really well for the band.

I was stoked because no other band wanted to play any of my tunes before. It's not that they weren't good, but I just never got the exposure. I showed them *Mr. Middle of the Road* and *I Want To Break My Heart Again*. Both of them liked the music and thought the rest of the guys would get behind it as well.

I didn't want to throw too much at them at one time, so I kind of held back some of my stronger tunes that I intended to present when everyone was together. I was thinking of two songs in particular that could be really cool for a club band. They were *Sleeping Giant* and *Carbon and Stone*. I had written *Sleeping Giant* about six months before the September 11th terrorist attacks on the World Trade Center and The Pentagon. Eerily, it deals with the same subject matter - the Palestinian conflict with Israel and how their hatred for each other draws others into their perpetual holy war. War is the *Sleeping Giant* about to be awakened. The lyrics go:

(First Verse)

Sleeping Giant – go back to bed

We all watch you rise

When you should close your eyes instead

(Chorus)

Sleeping Giant sleep away

Let us have our peace today

No one needs to feel the pain

A fragile monster gone insane

(Second Verse)

When he rises we'll all be gone

The only thing we learn

Is that the lesson still goes on

(Chorus)

(Third Verse)
Now your babies rest their heads
Trust is such a must
When they are safely in their beds
(Chorus)
(Fourth Verse)
I'm wishing well - all of those - opposed to me
Wishing them a grandchild
They can bounce upon their knee
(Chorus) Repeat – Fragile monster gone insane

I had the notion that the greatest weapon for peace was to wish your enemy a grandchild to bounce on his knee. The innocence of a child should never be dragged into a conflict. Perhaps hostilities could end for the sake of the children. I realized that I was just kidding myself, and I probably wouldn't receive the Nobel Peace Prize. But it's a good song anyway, so I still play it.

Mason and Mike picked up the chord progressions very quickly and then started putting some flesh on the bones with some blues licks and fills. I only had to sing, which was a real treat for a change. Usually when I play my music, I have to play a six-string guitar. Finally, I was free to play congas and sing with some other good musicians carrying the tune. Billie started to sing along and that made me feel pretty good. She's very particular how she uses the pipes these days. I'd have to honestly say that there were moments when the sound was so tight and harmonious that I was tempted to invite the band into a real studio instead of all the living-room product I'd been turning out for the past ten years.

When the music winded down, I got a similar sentiment from Billie, "You need to cut a CD and release that one Mack," she said of *Mr. Middle of the Road.* I wished that we had thought to set up a room recorder because the last take was pretty strong. *Oh, well, if it's meant to be, we'll get it again.*

Chapter Twenty

We had some God-awful health food for lunch. I'm sure it must have been good for me because it tasted terrible. I was thinking that I might have to make an excuse to get out of dinner and head over to Baker's Tavern for a pizza. The body can go only so long without a good slug of cholesterol washed down by liberal amounts of alcohol. I made a mental note to check out the fridge for any clues about dinner that looked like a recent purchase. If I saw anything that looked like a falafel or tofu, I was gonna' head out and get a flat tire or something. Some of the stuff Billie cooks is pretty scary. That lucky Victor; the trip to see his mother saved *his* ass.

Billie asked me if I wanted to bring a date for dinner, and I thought of Martie Coleman. I asked Mason if that would be mixing business with pleasure, and he said he didn't see why. He said if I liked her company, he didn't see a reason not to date her and that they probably wouldn't talk shop. I felt like I should have told him that she was miffed at him for talking to me about Uri, but I decided to just let it lie. It would be interesting to see whether or not she brought it up.

I called her office and invited her to dinner. She said she'd take a train from Sandy Hook to Clinton if I'd pick her up at the station. I told her I would and that I'd be glad to drive her home after dinner. Then she said, "You shouldn't drive after drinking, Mack."

"Well, then I guess you'll have to spend the night," I told her.

"Mason won't mind?" she asked.

"I'm sure he won't. It's a pretty big house, so I don't even think he or Billie will notice."

"Sounds like fun. I'll take the 5:20 train. It gets into Clinton at 6:05."

"I'll be there," I assured her.

Chapter Twenty-one

I told Billie there would be another guest at dinner, so I was committed to eat whatever healthy experiment she decided to come up with. I was thrilled to learn that she was actually being bad for once.

The menu was Chicken Cordon bleu done on a hot skillet with lots of butter and a little bit of oil. The chicken is pounded until tender and then rolled up with fatty Swiss cheese and imported Italian ham that is chock full of nitrates. Then the whole thing is wrapped in the chicken skin and seared in a very hot skillet to brown with the butter.

After baking for about fifteen minutes in a hot oven, she served the chicken over wild rice with carrots candied with brown sugar and a little bit of orange juice. I bought a couple bottles of some Louis Jadot Pouilly Fuisse, and for dessert we had Philadelphia style cheese cake, which is a little more creamy than New York style. I figured that the calorie count was somewhere around fourteen-hundred per person. It was a truly delicious meal. I never would have believed that Billie could cook something that does your body more harm than good. Maybe I wasn't adopted after all. Being Billie's brother is kind of confusing sometimes.

Dinner was full of animated anecdotes by Victor Reese about life in Hawaii and working with some of the world's most renowned astronomers. Indeed, he gave us the distinct impression that the brightest minds in the field never came back down to earth. Their minds were constantly in the stars. Victor made the comment that I reminded him of one of them. When he thought I wasn't paying attention, he asked me, "I'm not boring you, am I, Mack?"

"Oh, no, Victor," offered Billie. "Mack's never bored. He's taking it all in, believe me."

"He seems a million miles away," said Victor. He looked over at Martie and said, "Or perhaps he's falling in love with this lovely lady over here."

"Maybe," said Billie, "but Mack always acts like that. He's not zoning out, he's recording."

"Recording?" asked Victor.

"Mack has an eidetic memory," said Mason.

"What exactly is an eidetic memory?" asked Victor.

"Want to show him, Mack?" she asked.

"I guess," I answered.

Billie asked me, "Have you looked in the refrigerator since you've been here?"

"Yup," I told her.

Billie then said, "OK, Victor, go to the refrigerator and look inside."

Victor left the table and walked to the kitchen. He opened the refrigerator door and asked, "Now what?"

"Mack?" asked Billie, "Where is the horseradish?"

"Second shelf down – left side."

"The ketchup?"

"Top shelf – back right."

"Grape jelly," continued Billie.

"Bottom shelf – right side," I told her.

"Milk?"

"On the door," I said.

"Raspberry jelly?"

"Third shelf down – middle."

"Aw, I thought I had him on that one," she said.

"Enough!" said Victor. "I get it."

"Mack is really handy to have around," said Billie.

"Where are my keys, Mack?" she asked.

"I don't know," I told her.

"You don't know? Since when?" she asked.

"There are four sets of keys on the first floor of this house," I told her. "What do your keys look like?"

"Braided cowhide on the ring with turquoise beads and a silver Phoenix."

"They're hanging on a hook by the back door."

"That's incredible," said Victor.

"Actually, it can be a pain in the ass, Victor. There's a lot of stuff that I'd like to get out of my mind. Fortunately, most of it is only short-term memory. Still, I don't sleep so well sometimes."

"I've never seen anything like it," said Victor. "What's your secret? Is it photographic?"

"Not really," I told him. "It's more like auditory. When I want to memorize something I usually say it to my self, out loud, or imagine it being said by someone else. It works for music too. That's how a person plays by ear."

Everyone raved about the dinner, which made Billie purr like one of her cats. She likes nothing better than to please people. I think she missed her calling. Instead of being a singer she should have run a bed and breakfast.

Chapter Twenty-Two

We were so full, that we fell asleep on the couch watching a Florida Gator football game. I went to The University of Florida about fifteen years ago, so I had a good excuse to root for them. Martie told me she went to Georgetown, so we couldn't spark up any kind of rivalry. I figured it was just as well because I've lost more than one girlfriend that way.

We woke up at about ten thirty and decided to go for a late night constitutional. We walked down Billie's road, which is called Turkey-trot Road, to look at the stars. It's incredible how many stars are out there when you get away from all the city lights.

We saw a few meteors streak across the sky, and if I had to place a name on the mood of our evening, I suppose I would choose *romantic*. I wasn't looking for a romantic relationship, but I guess that's how they always come about. It always happens when you're not looking or supposed to be looking at something else. A little red flag jumped up in my mind and screamed *every time you pay attention to a woman, you kick yourself for not paying attention to something else.* I wondered what it would be this time. *Is it Mason I should be watching, or the band, or is it maybe even Martie herself?* I guessed I shouldn't try to save the world. Just let the future happen and try to shape it as it comes. That sounded like as good an excuse as any to treat myself to a little attention from a beautiful woman. I just couldn't shake the feeling that I was headed for a déjà vu all over again.

After driving Martie home to Sandy Hook, New Jersey, the next day, I got back to Hunterden county about 10:30 A.M. and caught Bill Riley, the band manager/security guard/NSA agent, just walking up the drive to Mason's house. He saw me drive in and stopped to talk to me. As I closed the door to the old VW that Mike was lending me, Bill said, "Nice car."

"It's Mike's," I told him.

"I used to have one just like it. It was a 1968 midnight blue bug. The thing used to run like a Porsche - not like this pig of a road hazard," he said referring to his aging Lincoln Town Car.

"Those were the days," I said not really knowing why. I couldn't help feeling out of the loop around Mason and his friends. I guess it was a little of my own medicine so to speak. When I'm involved in an investigation, I rarely take anyone else on board for fear that they might muck up the situation. That's all Martie was talking about when she told me to bug off, I guess, but it still hurts. I decided to cut through all the horse-pookie and said, "Bill, Mason told me that you're NSA."

"I know," he said naturally.

I mean, what *doesn't* he know being NSA right? I asked him, "Are you working in concert with Martie?"

"Not exactly. There's always a lot less cooperation between operatives from different government agencies than you might imagine."

"That's too bad. I think she's a pretty sharp lady," I then added, "in a lot of ways."

"Oh, you do, do you?" he asked, which kind of threw me off. *What does he know that I don't?*

"Is Mason home? Do you know?" he asked.

"I'm not sure, but I think so."

"Let's go find out," he said taking the lead and walking purposefully up the front steps to the door. He knocked loudly, and I wondered why he didn't ring the bell.

"I'm staying here, Bill. I have a key."

"I'm here to see Mason, Mack. I don't mean to be rude, but if he's not here, I'm not going in. You'll see why in time, I'm sure."

"Whatever," I said getting a little miffed. I went past him and tried the door. It was locked. I tried the bell and Bill said, "It doesn't work, Mack."

Mason came to the door and opened it, "Hi, Bill," he said. "Mack, don't you have a key?"

"Yeah, Billie gave me one. I was just about to use it when you came to the door."

"Well, come on in, guys. Can I get you a beer?"

"It's a little early in the day for me," I told him.

"I'll take one," said Bill. I guess some government jobs are better than others. I wouldn't mind being paid to drink beer at 10:30 A.M. But to be honest, I don't think I could get into it even if I *did* get paid. I struggle a little with alcoholism, so I try not to drink before 5:00 P.M. Mason and Bill popped a couple beers and acted like they were sharing a good joke. I got the distinct feeling that I was on the outside of the conversation, so I asked, "Do you guys want a little privacy?"

Mason got really serious for a moment and said, "No way, Mack. You're right in the middle of this, so I think you'd better stick around."

"By all means," said Bill. "Is Mack up to speed?" he asked Mason.

"Just about. But if we got a hit, I'm sure it'll be news to him, even though he's a regular in this kind of game."

"Just what the hell are you guys talking about?" I asked.

"You haven't checked it out?" asked Bill looking at Mason.

"I just got up," he said.

"Well, what are you waiting for? Let's get to it," said the NSA agent.

"Oh, yeah, don't let me stop you," I said even though I didn't have the slightest idea what I was talking about.

Mason went into his office and booted up his lap-top computer. On his hard-drive were all the programs that he could work on both at home and at the lab. The process that dealt with the different elements with which to dope a piece of glass was among them. The hard-drive also listed the last time the program was booted up. It said, 'today, 3:47 A.M.' Both Mason and Bill started to smile. Bill said, "Did you have a restless night last night, Mason?"

"Slept like a baby."

"Bingo," said Bill. "I guess Uri's got his program."

"Looks like it," said Mason.

I started to get the picture and felt a little sick to my stomach. "Martie lifted the program," I said rather drained.

"Just like Bill suspected she would," said Mason. "Don't take it personally, Mack. We couldn't tell you she was suspected of double ops. This merely confirms it. The program she lifted is junk."

"Glad to hear it," I said weakly. "So what does that make Martie, an enemy spy?"

"Not necessarily," said Bill. "She's got her own agenda, no doubt about that, but she might be acting on orders from her agency, which happens to be the Defense Department."

"Why didn't she just ask you for the program, Mason?" I just wasn't getting it.

"She will," said Mason. "Then she'll make sure that the two programs match up. She's afraid that I might be holding something back. Isn't that the way you see it, Bill?"

"That's right," said Bill calmly. "She's just covering her bases. Her job carries a lot of responsibility. I don't envy her if you want to know the truth."

"Somehow I feel a little used," I told them.

"I wouldn't, Mack. If she didn't lift the program here, she would have gotten it somewhere else. Actually it helps us. Now she's made the move, so we don't have to wait for it."

"But how did she know that the program was complete?" I asked. "You only told Victor about twenty-four hours ago that he could pick up the wire." Mason's eyes darted quickly from mine to the floor.

"They probably intercepted a phone conversation back to Hawaii," said Bill knowingly.

"But I heard you make Victor promise to keep it under his hat," I said.

"I'm sure he did. He probably only told his wife," said Mason. "I probably would have done the same thing."

"Where is Victor staying?" asked Bill casually.

"We don't know," said Mason just a little too quickly. "I'd be really surprised if someone managed to tap his phone on such short notice."

"You'd be amazed at the encroachment of civil liberties since the September 11th attacks," Bill told us.

"I don't think I even want to know," said Mason.

"Jesus," I said. "I think the cats are the only trustworthy entities in the whole state of New Jersey."

"No, Mack," said Bill seriously. "They work for me."

Chapter Twenty-three

Mason asked me if I wanted to go with him to the lab. The *real* lab - with the actual breakthrough he made on the process to manufacture the glass wire. I knew Victor was meeting him there, and I figured that he wanted to use me to smuggle the damned wire out. I was wrong again. The whole thing, all fifty feet of it, could have fit inside a shot glass. Victor put it between his cheek and gum like a pinch of chewing tobacco. I started to think New Jersey just got weirder every time you dared to turn over another rock. Mason sent Victor on his way and then told me that we had another gig.

"Good deal," I said. "All this cloak and dagger crap just reminds me of work. I came here for a change of pace."

"I hear ya'," said Mason. "Well, don't worry. It's over for now. As soon as Martie asks me for the process, I'm done."

"What happens when they learn that it doesn't work?"

"She'll come back and say that I compromised one of their operatives."

"Did you?"

"I don't think so. At least Bill doesn't think so. That's good enough for me."

"So when do you give Uri the false name of the guy working in Russia?" I asked him.

"It's all part of the program. It alludes to him by warning the NSA that Russia has three men capable of duplicating the process, and we can only count on one to perpetrate a stall. It also outlines the changes that would corrupt the doping process without alerting the other two competent scientists."

"So is Bill going to stop playacting as the band's manager?" I asked Mason.

"Who's playacting?" he said. "He gets the gigs for the band and then takes fifteen percent. He has a pretty good time at the gigs, plus he can use the money. The pay scale at NSA sucks." He started to laugh.

"You mean he intends to continue as the band's manager even though his assignment with Uri is nearly over?"

Mason starting laughing.

"What's so funny?" I asked him.

"Bill was our manager *before* his assignment to Uri. He's been getting us gigs for about a year." He laughed again.

"Man, this is a really messed up part of the country," I said. "I can't wait to go back down south where people are normal."

"Sure," said Mason. "At three-quarter's normal speed."

"Don't knock it if you've never tried it," I told him.

Chapter Twenty-four

I was really miffed at Martie Coleman. She played me for a complete fool. I knew she could have gained access to Mason's laptop on any number of other occasions, and that's what really hurt. It was like she was throwing it in my face. I decided to call her at her office. The receptionist said she was out of the office, so I left a message for her to call me on my cell phone. *Fat chance*, I thought. She'd gotten what she was after, so I assumed that our relationship would soon be over. I've never considered myself naive, but I was surprised to learn that operatives working for the United States government agencies would resort to sexual relations to expedite their assignments. I wondered if they qualified for hazard pay, given the prevalence of STD's, or sexually transmitted diseases. The whole subject was getting me pretty depressed, so I did what any other self respecting, mature individual would do. I went to Baker's Tavern to get drunk.

Buddy, the bartender, recognized me from the other night and brought me over a Bass ale. "First one's on the house," he said. I knew that wasn't really house policy, so I must have looked as miserable as I felt. He undoubtedly felt sorry for me in that psychic bartender kind of way and knew I was a friend of Peter and Gail. Friends in high places indeed. Their residence was actually right above us. I wondered whether the bar noises kept them up at night when they weren't in the mood to party.

After about the fourth round, I got a telephone call at the bar. Buddy brought me a cordless phone and said, "It's Mason."

"Thanks," I told him and answered the phone, "What's up, Mason?" I asked.

"I saw Mike's car out in front of Baker's on my way home. You okay?" he asked.

"Getting better all the time," I said.

"There was a message on my machine. Martie called."

"So?" I asked stubbornly.

"So, she doesn't want to talk to *me*," he said. "Why don't you give her a call?"

"Aren't you pissed at her for stealing your property?"

"Just because it walks like a duck and quacks like a duck, doesn't mean it's always a duck."

"What the hell is that supposed to mean?" I asked him.

"Call her, okay?" he asked.

"I'll call her," I said, and then handed the phone back to Buddy. "Can I settle up?" I asked him.

"No charge, Mack."

"Come on, Buddy. How much do I owe?"

"Mason said your money's no good here. Gail, too."

"Thanks, man," I told him placing a five dollar bill on the bar. "I'll see you later."

I sat in Mike's car in the parking lot and placed the call to Martie's office. The receptionist put me through, "Mack, I've missed you," she said. "Sorry I was out when you called."

"You've missed me, huh?" I asked sourly.

"Naturally," she said. "Last night was lovely."

"Is there something else I can do for you?" I asked sarcastically.

"Oh, yes," she said sleepily.

"Something else you need to download from Mason's laptop," I asked bitterly.

"I'm sure I don't know what you're talking about, Mack."

"I'm sure you do," I said.

"What was taken?"

"The program for the glass wire procedure at 3:47 A.M. Sound familiar?" I asked.

"I was in your arms at 3:47 A.M., Mack."

"That's what I thought until Mason booted up the program this morning."

"The program is a red herring, Mack. Why would I lift it if I knew it was a fake?"

"To compare it with the one Mason is supposed to supply you with."

"You're not making sense, Mack. It must have been Bill who lifted it to implicate me."

"Why would he do that," I asked.

"To get Mason to let his guard down, what little guard he has, anyway. He doesn't have any product, does he?"

"I'm not sure I should be telling you anything, Martie."

"Oh, I wish I was there," she said, *"so I could kick your ass you big, handsome dope.* Now tell me. Does he have any product, or not?"

"He gave a length to Victor for his telescope in Hawaii," I told her. I realized that Mason *doubted* her guilt as well when he asked me to call her. I was starting to believe her although I wasn't really sure why. Maybe I just wanted to believe in her because I didn't want what we had shared together to end.

"Did you talk about the wire in front of Bill?" she asked.

"Maybe a little," I said.

"Think, Mack. Did you mention the fact that Victor has a length of the wire?"

"Not directly, although I wondered why Bill asked us where Victor is staying."

"Jesus," she said. "We might be too late. Listen to me very carefully. I want you to meet me at the Park Center Complex in Hoboken. I'm taking the next ferry out of the city, and I'll meet you there. But first I want you to call Mason and tell him to get an address for Victor as soon as possible. Victor's life may hang in the balance. Don't ask any questions. Hang up the phone and do it now," she closed the connection.

I was a little shaken up by the call, but I managed to dial Mason and relay what Martie and I talked about. Mason said that her instincts were probably right on, but he had to wait until Bill made a move of some kind for fear of scaring him off. He told me he would try to get Victor's location from the observatory personnel in Hawaii. If that didn't work, he'd try to track down the address of Victor's mother. Meanwhile, I was pushing Mike's little VW for all she was worth. It indeed sounded a little like my Porsche as I winded through the gears. I could only hope that the little, air-cooled engine could handle the abuse.

Chapter Twenty-five

When I arrived at the Park Center Complex in Hoboken, Martie was waiting out front, standing next to the parking attendant. She waved me into the entrance and said to the attendant, "Robbie, this bug is gonna' take my space, so he doesn't need a ticket, okay?"

"Sure, Martie," said the attendant.

Martie hopped in the VW and said, "Drive up to the fourth level." When we got there she said, "Stop here. Then, when I pull out, pull in my spot, lock your car and get in mine."

I followed her instructions and ten minutes later we were screaming down the Garden State Parkway at about a hundred miles an hour. Martie was dressed in a navy blue pants suit with a white oxford button down shirt. On her feet were Reebok cross-trainers, and I noticed a pronounced bulge in her jacket just above her left breast. I asked her, "Since when do you carry a gun?"

"Since now," she said. "And, as of now, so do you." She handed me a 38 caliber, Smith & Wesson revolver and a handful of extra shells. I couldn't help commenting, "How quaint."

"I know," she said. "It belongs to my department head, Gerald Seiler. I think it was the original one issued to him about a hundred years ago."

"Does it work?" I asked only half kidding.

"You can bet your life on it."

"I think I just did," I told her.

I got the impression that she changed into those clothes at the Federal Building because it was a marked departure from the usual style of dress I had seen her in. She was all business now, and I have to admit the situation had me a little unsettled. She then told me, "I'm not sure what we'll be getting into when we find Victor, but I'll be damned if I'm gonna' get caught with my pants down."

"Oh, you're just trying to get me excited, Martie," I said.

"You'd better keep a cool head, Mack. There's a time and place for everything. Right now you need to focus."

I wasn't exactly sure what she was talking about, but I told her that I was up to any confrontation we might get into. All she could say was, "I hope so."

We were almost at the exit for Seaside Heights when she said, "I hope your hunch about Seaside is correct."

"We know his mother lives there, so he might be staying with her. Besides, we haven't heard from Mason, so that means that the observatory can't tell us where he's staying."

"Here's the exit; *now* what do you want me to do?" she asked.

"Head toward the beach," I told her.

"And your reasoning is?"

"Old lady, older house, sounds near the beach."

"I'll buy it," she said. "Maybe you should call Mason."

Just then my cell phone rang. Mason had the address, and it *was* near the beach. We found the house in less than ten minutes.

"Good work, Mack," she said. "It looks like he's here."

In the driveway were two cars. The one closest to the garage was a ten year old Mercury Marquis with faded blue paint. The second one looked like a late model rental car. I asked Martie, "So, what now?"

"I've got to go talk to him," she said.

"That's too bad," I told her. If Martie Coleman needed to talk to me about my safety, I'm sure it would ruin my day. "What's the plan?" I asked her.

"I'm open to suggestions," she said.

"You're the pro," I said to her. "Isn't there supposed to be a standard operating procedure for getting a targeted scientist safely to an airport?" I asked facetiously.

"As a matter of fact, there isn't," she said. Her irritation was evident in the tone of her voice. She clearly wasn't happy about the situation. What was implied, although left unsaid, was that she didn't think that fifty feet of wire was worth endangering all of our lives.

"Well, what do your instincts tell you?" I asked.

"We have to let it go down," she said.

"I don't understand," I told her truthfully.

"We can't make a stand and wait for them. I think Victor has to move to draw them out."

"The bait," I said.

"If you have a better idea. . ."

"I'm not criticizing, Babe. Tell me what to do."

"You have to follow us to Atlantic City Airport," she said.

"Us? As in you and Victor?" I asked.

"I'm going to try to ride with him undetected," she said. "I'll lie under a coat on the floor of the back seat."

"You really think we should divide our forces?" I asked. "Why not just both of us just ride with Victor and put him on the plane?"

"And then what happens when he gets to Hawaii?" she asked. "Hell, I'd like to go, but I'm pretty sure that my expense account ends at Atlantic City Airport."

"So you ride in the back seat of his car, and what do I do, exactly?"

"You follow us and run interference when the shit goes down."

"What the hell does that mean?" I asked a little shakily. "I'm afraid I've missed a few episodes of Mission Impossible."

"Just relax, Mack. Take a few deep breaths."

"Oh, that'll help," I said angrily.

"I'm serious, Mack," she said forcefully. "You're no good to me in the state you're in."

"Okay, okay," I said starting to take deep breaths. I felt kind of foolish and a little bit embarrassed.

"That's better," she said. "Don't worry, Honey. We'll get out of this, no problem."

I believed her. I could feel her confidence and it gave me confidence as well. Then she outlined her plan: "I expect Bill or Uri, or both of them, to make a move against Victor at the rental car return. Atlantic City Airport has a rental car return that's incredibly close to the terminal. It's literally feet from the door to the departure gate. It's the perfect place for an ambush. I've used it myself when I was with the DEA."

"You've ambushed drug smugglers at the rental car return of the Atlantic City Airport? What's that all about? Do you have nine lives or something?" I asked in amazement. "It's not as dangerous as you might expect. Most of the time they didn't even carry weapons. Think about it. They couldn't get them on the plane, whether they were leaving or returning."

"So what happens when they make their move?" I asked.

"I hope to surprise them by emerging from Victor's back seat. It would be nice to have a little cover when the time comes," she said.

"Yeah, provided I can find a parking space – provided they don't see me – provided I don't get arrested by the airport police. This whole plan is kind of cowboy if you ask me."

"Well, it's the easiest way to get them to make their move," she said. "That makes it a known. I'll take that any day against an unknown. That way you don't get shot in the back."

"I just hope we don't get shot in the front," I told her.

"You worry too much, Mack."

"Yeah, well, now I have someone to worry about beside myself," I told her.

"Well, Mack Willis. That's the sweetest thing anyone has ever said to me," she said batting her eyelashes.

"You need to get out more," I told her.

Chapter Twenty-six

Martie got out of her car and walked up to the door of Victor's mother's house. She was only inside for about ten minutes when she emerged with Victor in tow and loaded his bags into his rental car. She got in the back seat and soon disappeared from sight. Victor's mother didn't walk him out to his car to say good-bye.

They took the Parkway south toward Atlantic City, and I followed in Martie's sporty little Honda Prelude. I knew where they were going, naturally, so when we neared the airport, I drove on ahead and parked in the rental car return lot.

As far as I could tell there was no one there, lying in wait. *Perhaps I did worry too much*, as Martie said. I pulled into a space labeled Avis #12 and settled in to wait for Victor and Martie. After waiting about five minutes, I figured that Victor had stopped to top off the gas tank. A car entered the lot, so I slid down into my seat. I could hear it pull into the space next to me on the right, but I couldn't see any more than the top of the driver's side door without giving myself away. I was sure that I would be spotted when the driver got out. There was nothing I could do but wait. Nothing happened. The driver of the rental car next to me wasn't getting out of the car. Then I realized why. It must have been Bill and Uri. It was a simple matter to find out when Victor's flight was leaving. They could expect him to be returning his rental car about one hour before that.

Ten minutes passed and still there was no sign of Victor and Martie. I managed to snake my body between the front seats and into the backseat of Martie's car. Deciding to take a chance, I raised my head up just enough to see into the car next to me. There were two of them, and I could see that they were crouching down in their seats just as I had been. The whole situation might have been comical were it not for the certainty that the two men were dangerous. I heard another car enter the lot, and the two men dropped out of sight. I took that opportunity to sit up briefly and discovered that Victor had pulled into a space in the National Car Rental lot two rows over.

He got out and walked to the rear of his car and inserted the key into the trunk. There was no sign of Martie. I figured that she probably told Victor to proceed to the terminal as though there was nothing to be concerned about. I had to admire Victor's bravery. If I was expecting trouble in the car return lot outside an airport terminal, I would be moving much faster than he was. That, of course, would tip off Bill and Uri, and they would make their move at a later time. However, Victor played his part beautifully. He appeared to be alone like the lamb being led to slaughter. The two men quickly got out of their car. Victor was starting to walk toward the terminal when he spotted them. They trotted over and blocked his progress. When he realized that he wouldn't be able to get past them, he said, "You're Mr. Palmer, aren't you? I recognize you from the party in Bay Head."

"That's unfortunate, Dr. Reese. I'm afraid you're going to miss your plane back to Hawaii," said Uri.

"What are you talking about? Why are you treating me this way?" He put down his suitcase and looked around him for someone he could shout to. There was no one in sight.

"We want the wire, Doctor," said Bill Riley.

"I sent it on ahead to Hawaii," he lied.

"I doubt that very much," said Uri producing an automatic pistol from his belt. "Give me your car keys, now."

Victor handed over his keys, and the two men led him back to his car. They opened the trunk and made Victor climb inside. After throwing his suitcase in the back seat, Uri got in behind the wheel, and Bill Riley started back toward his car parked next to Martie's. I kept wondering where Martie was. Uri would have seen her if she was still hiding in the backseat of Victor's car. She must have gotten out when Victor started for the terminal. I was crouching down between Martie's car and the one to my left, wondering when Martie was going to make her move. I didn't have long to wait. I heard her yell, "It's over Riley," in my direction.

Riley spun quickly around and pulled his gun from the holster in his jacket. There was no one there. Martie had ducked down again after shouting to Riley. Uri got back out of Victor's car and slammed the door shut. "Bill?" he called out. "What's going on?" he asked.

"It's Coleman," said Riley.

"Shit," said Uri angrily. "Where is she?" he asked.

"How the hell should I know," he barked.

I raised my head up briefly and shouted, "It's over, Riley!" I was trying to draw them away from Martie's position, so she could choose a place to get the drop on them. Unfortunately, I got my wish. I heard Riley say, "That's that jerk, Willis. He's got to be behind those cars over there."

They started to separate and make their way over to where I was hiding. *Anytime, Martie,* I thought. *Draw them off of me please!* I could see Uri come into view, but I don't think he saw me before I backed up around the front of Martie's car. I rested the old revolver on the hood to rest the muscles of my arm. My right hand was holding the gun, and I noticed it was shaking slightly. That surprised me. I had been in a number of firefights in the past, and I don't ever remember my hands shaking. I started taking deep breaths.

All of a sudden, Bill Riley appeared on my left and raised his gun. "Hold it, Willis," he said, and I heard the hammer of his gun being pulled back. I reacted by instinct instead of any rational thought. If I had reasoned everything through and realized that he meant to shoot me, my actions would have been exactly the same. I dove to the ground after firing a round in Riley's direction. I knew it was only a matter of time before Uri would make his way around the car and then I would be assaulted from both sides. There was only one thing I could do. I had to pick a side and go. My only chance was to commit to one direction or another - cowboy it out and hope for the best.

The next twenty seconds were a blur of flashing images and loud noises. I chose to make my attack on Uri with the hope that Martie was watching and could somehow stop Riley from attacking me from the rear. I raised full up and jumped around the left, front fender of Martie's car. Uri was startled briefly and that gave me the chance that I needed. I raised the revolver and shot him in the chest. He dropped his gun and slumped against the side of the car. I quickly ran forward and kicked the gun away. I could see he was bleeding badly when I got close to him. I turned around to get a bead on Riley when I felt a burning explosion in my right shoulder. I'd been shot. I wanted to raise my gun but my arm felt like it was made of lead. I couldn't move it an inch. I was still clutching the gun, but it was hanging uselessly at my side. It was the same sensation that I'd had many times before in anxiety dreams, where someone is chasing me and my feet feel like they're moving through molasses. I could only stand there and anticipate the next shot from Riley. I was wondering where the bullet would strike me. *If it's a head-shot, will I hear it?* I remember wondering. Then I heard Martie's voice again, "Watch your back, Riley!" she shouted. She was crouched in a shooter's stance about forty feet away. Her hands remained rock steady as she trained the gun on Bill Riley. Then she said, "You'll lose, Riley, if you try it."

Riley made his move anyway. He spun around quickly and raised his gun at Martie. Fire exploded from the muzzle of her gun in rapid succession as she put four bullets in Riley's chest before she realized that the first one hit her target. She remained in her stance long after Riley's body fell to the pavement. I got to my feet and yelled, "Martie! I'm over here." Martie didn't move. She kept her gun trained on Bill Riley's lifeless form, lying in front of her car. "Don't move," she said. I watched her slowly make her way up to Riley's body and kick the gun out of his hand. Only then did she relax her posture and walk toward me. "How bad is it?" she asked me noticing the bloodstain growing on my shoulder.

"You tell me," I said. I was starting to feel a chill even though it was at least sixty-five degrees. Martie went over and checked Uri for a pulse. Then she came over to look after me. I noticed that Martie's hands were shaking badly. I asked her, "Are you okay?"

"I'm fine," she said. "I shake every time I fire my weapon, but only *after* I fire my weapon." She gently eased my jacket off and said, "It looks like the bullet went right through your shoulder."

I was determined not to act like a weenie and pass out, but I had to concentrate. I noticed my hands were still shaking also. I came to the conclusion I was concerned for Martie's safety and that's why my hands were shaking during the firefight. I wanted to tell her that was the reason, when she said, "Lie down on the backseat of my car, Mack. If you pass out, I don't want to have to pick you up. I'm gonna' call 911."

"What about Uri?"

"He's gone," she said. "It's weird, but just before he went he seemed to smile at me," she said. "Why would he do that?"

"I guess there are worse ways to die," I told her.

"And worse times as well," she said. I noticed that her hands had stopped shaking, but she had tears in her eyes.

"What was her name?" I asked.

"What?" she asked wearily.

"The woman at the train station - the one who was killed. What was her name?"

"Michelle."

"Did you love her?" I asked.

"I got her the job, Mack," she said wiping her eyes.

"I'm so sorry, Martie."

"Yeah, well, so am I."

Chapter Twenty-seven

Victor made his flight back to Hawaii. We let him out of the trunk and told him to go to the rental car office like nothing ever happened. Martie was tempted to just leave the bodies in the parking lot and drive me to the hospital, but her sense of decency forced her to wait for the airport police to respond to the gunshots and file the customary reports to justify deadly force among the civilian population. My wound made the claim of self-defense much more believable. Martie said that her office had been monitoring Bill's activities over the past six months and was well aware of his association with Uri and Dimitri. They felt that it was only a matter of time before either Uri or Bill Riley would force a confrontation. They knew that Mason's research would remain out of reach despite his clumsy attempts to pacify Uri with descriptions of his progress.

Martie knew Mason was an amateur and would make a critical mistake sooner or later. She was relieved that the threat they posed was no longer a problem. She felt no remorse for killing Bill Riley. He would have killed her in a heartbeat if he had the chance. But Uri's death was a different matter. She asked me if I was upset about it, and I told her no. I made a choice to take the offensive position, and it saved my life. I imagine that she asked the question because she was the one to look him in the eye at the time of his death.

Martie finally got out of Atlantic City Airport around 6:00 P.M. and picked me up at Atlantic City Hospital. We drove to her house in Sandy Hook, and I slept for about ten hours. When I woke up, I discovered that she had been cooking for about three hours and had a lot of fancy treats wanting to spoil me. She fed me quiche with spinach and bacon surrounded by pineapple chunks with Mandarin orange slices. The coffee was vanilla macadamia nut from a specialty shop in the Sandy Hook Mall, and for dessert, she served an apple cinnamon crumb cake with French vanilla ice cream. I asked her why she was spoiling me with all the fancy food, and she just said, "Every time I have a close call, I like to demonstrate how good it is to be alive. You just lucked out by happening to be staying here at the time."

Chapter Twenty-eight

Victor called Mason about six days after he arrived back in Hawaii. He wanted to assure him that he had destroyed the wire according to Mason's instructions.

"What happened with your experiment?" asked Mason.

"Oh, it was a success, of sorts. The wire delivered a rather unexpected collection of data."

"What do you mean?" asked Mason.

"Well, I've received a strong signal of x-ray and gamma radiation from every quadrant that I focused on. However, the data seemed to be identical no matter where I concentrated the equipment. Unless I can find a cipher to the patterns, I'll have to conclude that it's merely a collection of "black noise," or meaningless static that appears to be a constant throughout the cosmos."

"That's too bad," said Mason. "I know that you had high expectations for the application of the wire to your observations."

"It's not a failure, Mason. It's information that we didn't have before you helped us out. I still appreciate your cooperation, and I'll keep you informed as to any further discoveries with respect to the cipher."

"Thank you, Victor," said Mason. "It was my pleasure to help."

When Mason told me about Victor's call, I was a little put off. I know it wasn't Victor's fault, but two men died trying to steal the damned wire from him on his way to Hawaii. Now it seemed that they died for static. Cosmic *black noise*, no less. Maybe it was an easy way out for Uri. He had something pretty bad going on in his body. I imagine it was painful, and he existed on painkillers most of the time. That was why he was sick to his stomach during the party at Bay Head. Mason said that he was dying, but he never elaborated on the subject. I didn't talk much about the shootout at the airport. Mason acts a little flippant about the people he affects with his work. But I have to hand it to him; he abandoned his work on the wire. He saw the ramifications of creating a space-based laser with an EMR concussion application by boosting the signal to a plus-light speed. He knows it's just a matter of time before someone else picks up where he left off, but he says he's sleeping very well, *thank you very much*. I guess that's something he's been struggling with, although he never mentioned it.

Martie flew to Florida with me where I planned to recover from my shoulder wound. I found playing the congas pretty painful, so I had to beg off from playing with the band. I still gave them a half-dozen of my tunes, and they turned out pretty good. They cut a nice CD and are currently getting a fair amount of airplay on a local college radio station. Who knows? Maybe I'll actually get some royalty checks from the CD sales. I'm not sure he took me seriously when I suggested that he change the name of the band from Blue Cactus to Dark Matter. Not many people take me seriously. My ex-wife Susan certainly didn't. As far as Martie Coleman goes, I guess only time will tell.

Part Two

Dark Matter

Chapter One

D r. Reese peered over the rim of his wine glass at the shapely young grad student seated across the table. She, too, was sipping on a glass of dark wine that matched her eyes, which reflected the flame of the candle before them. Theirs was a world of light and reflection. They mapped the heavens from an observatory fourteen thousand feet above the beautiful blue Pacific on the big island of Hawaii.

The mountain was named Mauna Kea, and the grad student was named Sidney Peel. She was in love with her mentor, Dr. Victor Reese, and had been since she first laid eyes on him. It wasn't his looks that drew her to him or any kind of skill he possessed with regards to words or gestures. In fact, it was just the opposite. His quiet, sober disposition only enhanced the understated mystery that spoke to the fact that Dr. Reese was a man with a secret.

Sidney Peel could feel that Victor understood the stars and their endless journey through time itself more personally than any other astronomer she had ever come in contact with. The stars were Victor's friends. He liked to keep a close eye on his friends, and from some good advice, an even closer eye on his enemies. Asteroids were his enemies. One in particular stole his sleep as well as his hope for humanity until just the night before last.

"You've changed," said Sidney. Her dark hair fell across her shoulder in a lazy curve that seemed to tease the eye into falling on her ample breasts. They seemed to struggle with the third button of her silk blouse, which made Victor all the more aware of the good things in life he had been missing. He had been purposely avoiding things like the taste of a good wine or the company of a beautiful woman. Until the night before last he could only mourn the tragic loss of their passing. Victor was the only man on Earth who knew of its imminent destruction.

An asteroid had been racing toward our beloved planet at over sixty thousand miles per hour. It was four miles across and seven miles long; a wayward piece of a comet that had passed through our solar system a mere century before. But the good news is, *it has moved.* To the good doctor's tremendous relief and delight, it is no longer where it is supposed to be. Certainly a reason for celebration, hence the dinner date with the lovely Ms. Peel.

"What do you mean I've changed?" he asked her.

"Well, for starters, the fact that you accepted my invitation to have dinner with me. That's a first."

"A fact of which I am truly remorseful, I assure you. Anything else?" he asked her.

"Well, this afternoon you smiled at me. That's why I asked you out tonight. I'd just about given up on you, and then you suddenly gave me hope."

"Hope is a wonderful thing, Sidney."

"There, you called me Sidney, not Ms. Peel. That's a first too."

"And will you call me Victor?"

"Yes, Victor. Will you tell me what's come over you? Not that I'm complaining or anything. I think it's wonderful."

"Yes, Sidney I will tell you, and it is wonderful. In fact, I can show you, in that you are a scientist. You're one of the few people who could understand."

"You're so mysterious, Victor. I'm sure that's what I see in you, why I'm attracted to you."

"That has a lovely sound to it, and yet a few days ago it would have only made me sad."

"What on Earth are you talking about, Victor."

"Oh, it's nothing on Earth, Sidney. And with a little bit of luck, it never will be."

"I don't understand," she said.

"You will. And then you will cry as I did."

Martie was a really good sport about me sticking my nose into government business. She actually ended up saving my life during a nasty firefight in a car-return parking lot at the Atlantic City Airport in New Jersey. I was shot in the shoulder, but luckily the bullet went clean through without hitting any bone. Even so, I can't imagine how it could have been more painful.

We were escorting a scientist, actually an astronomer named Victor Reese, to his flight back to Hawaii. He was carrying a small coil of fiber-optic wire that my brother-in-law Mason had invented, which can boost a light source beyond light speed. Victor wanted the wire to boost very small radio waves to measurable values.

As it turned out, a couple of Russian black-ops thieves were bird-dogging Victor the whole time he was in New Jersey. We were on the lookout for them, but they managed to ambush us anyway. They wanted the wire to boost the intensity of a "pulse laser" used to create EMR or electromagnetic radiation concussion values. It seemed that people were not satisfied fighting their wars here on earth – they wanted to do so from space. No matter what you invent, I guarantee you that someone will find a way to kill someone with it.

To this day I'm not sure just how much luck as opposed to skill allowed us to overcome the Russians at the airport. They died in the firefight. As a former homicide detective, and current P.I., it wasn't the first time I ever had to shoot a man.

Regardless of what you hear, it never gets any easier. Every time is like the first time. It sucks the life out of the shooter as well. I'm not sure just how much life I've got to lose, so I'm having serious thoughts about getting out of the game for good. So is Martie. She works for the Defense Department, and although she'd never admit it, she's part of black ops. But I'm not giving up on her just yet. We've shared some pretty good times when we weren't getting shot at.

Martie flew down to Florida with me for a couple of weeks while I began my physical therapy. As it happens, I ended up putting it off for one reason or another because things just kept popping up to distract me. Things like trying to make a living for instance.

Chapter Two

My shoulder was killing me. I was supposed to go to the rehabilitation clinic at the Easter Seals complex, but decided I could handle the job myself in my swimming pool. I was wrong. It was starting to stiffen up and with each measure of lost movement came more pain. "Jesus," I said to Martie, "I must be getting old. It never used to take me this long to bounce back after an injury."

"It was a pretty serious wound, Mack."

"I know, but still . . . where are those painkillers?"

"Easy boy. You don't want to end up like Rush Limbaugh."

"Not a chance, Martie. I grew up in the sixties," I told her.

"So did he," she said.

"He must not have paid much attention."

"Did you call Susan?" she asked referring to my secretary.

"Not yet. She'll make me go to work."

"Bull-*shit*," she said forcefully. "Not for at least a week."

"I don't mean real work. I mean just busy work. You know, collecting money from stingy old ladies. There's a couple of old birds up in Palm Beach who need to throw money at me before they die or something. Tell me something, why are all the rich ones so cheap?"

"Who knows? Maybe they think they'll live forever. Maybe they should hang around Victor," she said and then was immediately sorry. I could tell that the shootings had sucked a little life out of her as well.

~

By a strange coincidence, we got a call from Victor that evening. We had just finished dinner, but it was only one o'clock Victor's time. Although he sounded very excited, his call turned out to be an unfortunate harbinger of possible doom.

"I have to find Mason," he said urgently.

"Have you tried his home in New Jersey?" I asked.

"Of course," he said. "That's the first place I called. Then, I called Bell Labs and Mike said he'd gone off surfing somewhere."

"He does that a lot," I said.

"Do you have a number for his cell phone? I can't find Billie either," he said.

Billie is Mason's wife, and she's also my sister. She often goes with Mason on his surfing trips to Barbados. She doesn't surf, but she likes to cook a lot of exotic foods with the locals. I told Victor, "I'm not sure he'd have his phone turned on in Barbados."

"Well, do you know where he's staying?" he asked.

"Trust me, Victor. I've seen the pictures of where he stays, and they don't have a phone. They don't have a refrigerator or electricity if I remember correctly. What's the big deal?" I asked him. "Why do you have to find Mason?"

"I have to get another section of his glass wire."

"But you told us that all you got was static or *black noise*," I told him.

"I lied to you, Mack. I lied to all of you."

"What's this all about, Victor?" I was getting a little pissed at this point.

"It wasn't just static," he said pitifully. "I got a message. Actually a series of messages, from . . . space, from . . . everywhere."

"What kind of messages?"

"It was all bad news, Mack. That's why I didn't say anything. But all that's changed, I think."

"What the hell are you talking about?" And then he told me. He had found a pattern to all of the *black noise* and was actually able to decipher a message from the dark matter. Amazingly, the message was the same from any point of dark matter that he examined. He didn't have to tell us that the odds of that happening were beyond astronomical.

Victor operates one of the largest telescopes in the world perched atop Mauna Kea, which is a mountain on the big island of Hawaii. It turned out that the *black noise* made references to specific mass values and vectors. In short, meteors. Each meteor was given a value and a specific mass and vector in time and space. Victor discovered the message by abandoning the linear sense of time and moving forward and backward relative to the changing mass values in each vector. He traced a life extinction event to the Yucatan Peninsula exactly sixty-five million, two hundred thousand, nine hundred and eighty-one years ago. It was the impact that wiped out the dinosaurs on earth. A similar mass value was assigned to the Shoemaker-Levy comet that crashed into Jupiter in the year 2001. That one had the power of ten thousand Hiroshima bombs.

When Victor followed the projection forward, he discovered the sad fact that the earth was due for another life extinction event in our lifetime.

He made the discovery about the asteroid with the use of a length of very special fiber optic wire developed by my brother-in-law Mason Spender. The wire actually boosts the signal beyond light speed, which enables Victor's telescope to receive images as small as half-a-photon. When Victor trained his telescope on various sections of supposedly *dark matter*, he found that it wasn't really dark after all. What was even more interesting was that the radio waves weren't as random as he expected them to be. They repeated a pattern, which contained a message. *The same message*, no matter where he aimed the telescope. At first he told us that it was just random *"black noise,"* and, although interesting, it was of no particular significance. It was, in fact, the biggest lie in the history of mankind.

The messages were a series of vectors and corresponding mass values. Thus, the size and path of over a thousand NEA's or *near Earth asteroids* that could be tracked forward and backward in time.

Apparently all intelligent life across the cosmos has the same idea or agenda. They realize that space travel to other worlds is impossible due to the incredible distances involved, so they communicate the only information worthy of transmission, namely, *collision warnings*.

We asked him why he didn't try to warn the people of Earth, so they might try to alter the path of the meteor. Victor just laughed, and said, "It's Shoemaker-Levy's big brother."

"Holy Jesus, help us all," I said.

"He may have," said Victor.

"What are you talking about?" I asked him.

"It's moved," he said excitedly.

"What? The asteroid?"

"Exactly."

"Moved where?" I asked hopefully.

"Well, I'm not exactly sure, but I know it's not where it's supposed to be. Do you know what that means?" he asked.

"That it's not going to slam into the earth?"

"Yes, I'm hoping that's exactly what it means."

"How do you know it has moved?" I asked him.

"Because it should have slightly altered the gravitational field of Xeries on a recent fly-by."

"You're sure?" I asked, *as if I had any idea what the hell Xeries was.*

"Absolutely. However, I'll need another section of wire to be sure, but as of now, go ahead and buy green bananas."

I was beginning to think that *he* was bananas, but I have to admit he scared the bejesus out of me. He said he hadn't told us that the fateful event would occur, largely, because he figured that there was nothing we could do about it. Victor had also chosen not to share this information with the rest of humanity, and I don't blame him for his decision. I, for one was no better off with the knowledge that the world could end in my lifetime. I'm sure I would have been better off not knowing. Martie felt the same way. At least we had the slim hope that the situation had changed. Victor was convinced that the orbit of the asteroid had significantly changed. He was almost positive that it no longer poses a threat to earth. *"Almost,"* was a word I consequently came to despise. I gave him Mason's cell phone number and made him promise to keep us informed as to whether or not it was the end of the world. I'm sure the sarcasm went right over his head, but I thought it had a nice ring to it.

The knowledge was kind of a double-edged sword. On the one hand our lives were more precious to us, and we were sure not to waste any time that we had left. On the other hand, we couldn't help feeling saddened by the knowledge that all the beautiful things around us could be so temporary. I guess that life goes on as they say, only possibly not on Earth. I could only hope that we treated our next world better than we had treated this one.

It made us feel that possibly God was talking to us through Mason's laser and we would do well to live our lives in accordance with His wishes. I was ready to strike a deal that if God would give us back our world, I would make a conscious effort to be a better human being.

Chapter Three

Ithas almost a week since we'd talked to Victor Reese in Hawaii, so we decided to call him after dinner. Nine o'clock in Florida was only four on the big island, so we placed the call to the observatory. He wasn't in, and when we reached his research assistant, we learned that he was once again in New Jersey.

"So far, so good," said Martie. She was just what I needed. I was in a dark funk after learning the bad news from Victor, and I just couldn't shake it. Martie was a rock. I couldn't let her actually take the news braver than me, so I had to project an outward appearance that was somewhat less than truthful. The truth was I was scared and depressed. I didn't want to die before I managed to make something of myself. Sure, maybe I helped a few people get along a little better if there was any kind of dough in it, but that doesn't count. I'd written a bunch of songs, but I seemed to remember a cliché used to describe anything nearly worthless as, "you could buy it for a song." I guess to be truthful, the phrase refers to someone singing the song, not actually writing it, but you know what I mean. I just wasn't ready to go out with a bang until I did something noble. It was really starting to get to me, so I started goofing with Martie to try to get her goat and at the same time cheer myself up.

When she laid down for a quick nap, I made this entry into her journal: *Mack Willis is an extraordinary private investigator. He just doesn't know it yet. I saw his potential the first time I met him. It was at a very large party in a town called Bay Head on the*

New Jersey shore. He discovered a Russian mole that was working with some of the members of the band Blue Cactus, who were chemical engineers, no less. The band was just a hobby with most of them, but Mack, also being an excellent conga player, took it a little more seriously. To make a long story short, he was instrumental in bringing down the infamous mole Uri, along with a highly placed NSA agent named Bill Riley, who was also a Russian spy.

These men had established cover identities for nearly a decade, and Mr. Willis managed to end their careers in his spare time while on vacation playing congas in his brother-in-law's band.

I was merely lucky enough to accompany him during the apprehension phase of the operation, which took place at the Atlantic City Airport car-return parking lot. I was granted a two-week leave of absence from The Department of Defense where I was currently employed. I decided to follow Mr. Willis to his home in Florida to learn more about a recent case of his, which involved another group of Russians in league with a terrorist cell from Afghanistan..."

"Mack! Just what the hell do you think you're doing?"

"Martie . . . " I said as she caught me by surprise. "I thought you were sleeping."

"What are you doing with my laptop?" she demanded.

"Just making a little entry in your journal," I tried not to look guilty and failed.

"What *kind* of entry? Let me see it." She took the laptop from me and scrolled through the entry. "What a complete load of horse shit," she barked. "I saved your life in that parking lot, you sorry-son-of-a-bitch!"

"Take it easy, Martie. I was just kidding, okay?"

"No, it's not okay. Just stay the hell away from my laptop, you got it?" she fumed.

"All right," I said. "Geeze, I thought you'd get a kick out of it."

"Well I didn't. What if someone else read it? You make me sound like a gushing schoolgirl."

"Well, aren't you?" I asked facetiously.

"The only thing gushing around here is your ego, Willis. I can't believe I ever let you get involved in your brother-in-law's case. Now I feel responsible for your shoulder wound. I never should have let you come with me."

"It's a damn good thing you did, or else you'd be dead right now." I told her seriously.

"I don't know how you figure that," she said. "I could have handled the situation very well without your interference."

"I can't believe what I'm hearing. There were *two* of them, Martie. That's two guns against one."

"Uri was an amateur, and he had a death wish. He committed suicide by cop. It happens all the time."

"First of all, I'm not a cop," I corrected her. "Not anymore. And, second of all, you're not invincible, Martie. You'd better come to terms with that, and soon. You may not have me around next time."

"Puh-lease, Willis. I better not have you around when I'm working. The only time I want to be around you is when you're either feeding me or making love to me, got it?"

"Okay. Get out the handcuffs, missy."

"Believe me, I will. As soon as your shoulder wound heals."

Chapter Four

Martie and I drove to Palm Beach to collect some fees and have lunch on Worth Avenue. Susan, my secretary, insisted that I catch up on her back pay as well as her alimony payments, thus the need to go to Palm Beach. That's right, you guessed it. Susan is also my ex-wife. I've decided not to volunteer that little bit of information to Martie for the time being. A short time ago I learned the hard way that girlfriends and ex-wives should never be allowed to compare notes. There's usually only one loser in that scenario, yours truly.

Lunch was a Caesar salad and some sushi, which reminded me of my first date with Martie. We shared a bonsai roll at the sushi bar inside the World Financial Center in New York City. Martie's office is across the street in the Federal Building. The sushi on Worth Avenue is the better of the two. After lunch I called a woman named Emma Sinclair whose daughter Cynthia decided to run away with her gym teacher and take up residence in a Miami Beach hotel. The gym teacher's name was Misty McCord, so Mrs. Sinclair asked me to be discreet about my investigation. I tracked them down and brought the girl back in a little more than a week and gave Emma a bill for three grand. She had already given me a fifteen-hundred-dollar retainer, so it made for a pretty good week.

How was I supposed to know she'd take off with Misty again a week after I brought her back. Anyway, a deal's a deal so I was determined to collect the dough. God, I love Palm Beach. I just wouldn't want to live there.

We arrived at the Sinclair house about two in the afternoon. They had a real live butler who buttled us into Emma's parlor and asked us if we wanted anything to drink. I didn't want to disappoint him so I asked for a beer. Martie passed on the drink and began taking in the artwork on the walls. When the butler left the room, she asked me, "Tell me these paintings are not the originals,"

"Probably," I said.

"You didn't charge her enough," she said.

"*Now* you tell me. Where were *you* when I was billing her?" I asked sourly.

"Babysitting your brother-in-law," she said.

Emma Sinclair made a somewhat dramatic entrance by handing over my beer on a sterling silver tray and saying, "I've just taken over Edward's duties, Mr. Willis. Here is your beer."

"You make a very attractive butler, Mrs. Sinclair," I told her.

"Why, thank you. Are you going to introduce me to this lovely young woman?" she asked gesturing to Martie.

"*Young woman?* Oh, Mack! I *like* her," said Martie laughing.

"May I present Ms. Martie Coleman," I said. "Martie, this is Emma Sinclair."

"How do you do," said Martie extending her hand, ever the proper lady *in disguise*.

"Let me tell you why I called you, Mr. Willis," said Emma. This threw me for a loop. I thought I'd called her. I was *sure* I called her. I caught Martie smiling and holding back a laugh.

"You have some wonderful paintings, Mrs. Sinclair," said Martie.

"Please, call me Emma, Martie. You see? That's the whole

point. Now I have one less."

"You're missing a painting?" I asked. Nothing gets past me when I'm really tuned in.

"A Picasso. It's called The Old Guitar Player."

"Was it stolen?" I asked. I was on a roll now.

"Well, I don't think it was misplaced for God's sake. It was on loan to the school when suddenly it was gone."

"The school?" I asked.

"The art school at the Norton."

I did my brick imitation rather successfully.

"The Norton Art Museum on Olive Street," she said. "They have an art school on the premises and often borrow paintings from the community for the students to study. It's quite an opportunity to have so many fine examples in the area. They were studying Picasso's blue period, so naturally I leant them The Old Guitar Player."

"Naturally," I said. I catch on fast.

"So will you find it?" she asked me.

"Mrs. Sinclair. I'm here to collect the balance of my bill. I've brought a copy in case you've misplaced the one I gave you."

"Whatever," she said. "I'll write you a check. But what about my Picasso? Will you take the case?"

"Sure," I said.

"He can't," said Martie rather quickly.

"Martie, this could get cold pretty fast. I've got about two days to get a lead, or else we might as well *fuh-gedda-boud-it*." I did my best New Jersey accent rather poorly.

"Mrs. Sinclair," began Martie. "Mack has recently had a serious accident, and the doctor has required that he rest for at least two weeks."

"I'll take the case."

"Damn it, Mack!"

"I'll work on it for two days, and if I come up empty, no charge," I told her.

"And your fee if you recover it?" asked Emma.

"Ten thousand sound okay?" I asked.

"That's a lot of money for two days work."

"How much is the painting insured for?" I asked.

"I'll write you a check," she said. "If you can't find the painting, just deduct your previous bill and send me the balance."

Martie was smiling again even though she was mad at me. "Why are men so stubborn, Emma?" she asked.

"Are they?" asked Emma. "I thought they were just greedy."

"Yeah, that too," Martie said screwing her eyes up at me.

Chapter Five

When we were leaving the Sinclair house, Martie made the observation that I hadn't really been paid for my services rendered. If I recovered the painting then I was due the full ten thousand she had given me for a retainer. I still had fifteen hundred coming and a sneaky-suspicion that Emma was likely to stiff me. I told Martie that if I found the painting, I'd send Emma the eighty-five hundred and then hold it for ransom for the other ten. She told me I'm a lousy businessman. Most women tell me that.

~

I called the gallery on my cell phone and asked to be connected to the gift shop. A woman answered and I found out that they were open till five-thirty. I knew that Martie was still mad at me because I noticed that she wasn't talking very much. *Oh, well, as long as I'm her ride she has to play along, right?*

The woman in the gift shop seemed very nice at first. Her name-tag read, Mrs. Bell, but no first name. I introduced myself and asked her what she thought were the best paintings that were "up." She just about told me it was none of my business. She said that she didn't have time for idle chatter. *Very interesting*, I thought. What the hell else did she have to do except talk to the patrons? Here was a woman who clearly didn't like her job. She was stuck in the little shop day-in and day-out, without the slightest interest in discussing the very thing that provided her livelihood, namely, *art*. I noticed that the store sold art supplies as well as post cards and prints of all the museum exhibits. When I asked her if many students shopped there, she was also somewhat evasive. She asked me if I needed any help finding anything so I told her, "I'm looking for a print of The Old Guitar Player."

She froze for an instant and then said, "I don't think we have that particular print in stock."

"It's a painting by Pablo . . ."

"I know who it's by," she barked at me.

"Did you know that it was on display here at the museum?" I asked her.

"It was displayed at the school," she said. "Not the museum."

"Did you see it?"

"None of your business," she said pointedly.

"Did you steal it?" I asked. Again she stood frozen for a second.

"What did you say?" she asked.

"I said, did you know it was missing?" she didn't know what to say. I was sure that she had learned of the theft, so why not just admit that she heard about it. *Why not indeed, unless, of course, she stole it?* I was beginning to imagine that I had just earned the easiest ten thousand dollars of my life when she said, "I heard about the theft. It was an atrocity."

"Why do you say that?" I sensed that she was finally going to open up.

"This particular theft must have been commissioned by a private collector who never intends to display it."

"Too hot? Is that what you mean?"

"Naturally. News travels very fast in the art world, Mr. Willis. If anyone were to display Emma's Picasso, he would be immediately guilty of accepting stolen property."

I had introduced myself as Mack, not Mack Willis. "You know Mrs. Sinclair? And how do you know my name?"

"Emma Sinclair is my sister," said Mrs. Bell. "Do you think you can help her recover the painting?"

I noticed Martie struggling not to laugh and said, "Maybe you can help me, Mrs. Bell. Do you know of any students who are struggling to keep up with either their studies or their tuition?"

"Just about all of them," she said. "This is a very difficult school."

"Do you suspect anyone?"

"You're the detective, Mr. Willis. Well, go ahead and detect something."

Martie's giggling was starting to piss me off. Finally, I said, "Well, there isn't much to go on, is there?"

"Sure, there is," said Mrs. Bell. "The thief had to be someone employed by the school, but not any of the instructors. They have too much respect for the painting and the whole concept of sharing it with the world. Did you know that if a tree falls in the forest and no one is there to hear it, it doesn't make a sound?" she asked.

"I've heard that," I told her.

"So if it wasn't one of the instructors - and it wasn't one of the students. . ."

"Wait a minute," I said. "Why couldn't it have been one of the students?"

"No opportunity," said Mrs. Bell. "The painting was taken on Saturday morning when the school was closed. No students are permitted at the school on weekends. Every doorway is locked with those roll-down, steel, cage doors," she said motioning to the one that locked up the gift shop after hours.

"What about a custodian?"

"There aren't any. The students have to do double duty as housekeeping."

"So, if it wasn't a teacher - and if wasn't a student or a custodian, who's left?" I asked.

"No one," said Mrs. Bell. "That's why my sister called a private detective. It's a mystery."

"Actually, I called her," I said noticing Martie's silly grin. She seemed to really get a kick out of any time I was confused. Some women are cruel sometimes.

Chapter Six

When we got back to my car, Martie asked me, "What do you think?"

"The painting's still at the school."

"You know it's not," she said.

"I know they claim it's not. I know they think it's not; however, I'm still not convinced it's not. Look at the evidence. There was no opportunity for those with a motive and no motive for those with an opportunity. Therefore, it didn't happen, yet." I told her.

"What do you mean, yet?" she asked.

"You'll see."

We headed back to Deerfield Beach where my little house is located and took a nice long nap. My shoulder was still stiff, and I was running out of painkillers fast. I knew it was only a matter of time before I would actually have to do some real exercises in the pool. I knew it would hurt, so I put it off as long a possible. When we woke up, I took two more pills and got Martie to walk the beach with me for a while.

As soon as I felt the pills start to kick in, I took a tentative dip in the ocean. There were no waves to speak of, and the water was a soothing seventy-four degrees. Martie said, "I can't believe how warm this water is. We would never swim this time of the year in New Jersey."

"The salt is good for my shoulder," I said.

"How does it feel," she asked me.

"Like shit," I admitted.

"You've got to do the exercises, Mack."

"I know. I can think of one right now that I should be doing. Would you like to help me?"

"Sure," she said.

"Okay, let's go back and do some twelve-ounce curls," I said referring to twelve-ounce bottles of beer.

"You're a lousy patient, Mack Willis."

"Yes, but I'm good at other things."

We sat on my couch and watched golf for a while. I was feeling kind of bold so I stole a few kisses, and then we went out for a pizza. It turned out that we both had the same taste for New York style with sausage and mushroom. Things were definitely starting to look up in our relationship. I've had affairs based on a lot shakier things than kisses and pizza. Martie Coleman was a hell of a lot of fun to hang out with. Too bad she was ticked off at me for working. I guess she only had my welfare in mind. I knew I would heal sooner or later, especially if I could get a hold of some more of the pills that took me to la-la land. When I took two of them, I could move my shoulder pretty well and not even scream. In fact, I was feeling well enough for a drive to Miami.

Chapter Seven

"Miami?" asked Martie. "Whatever for?"

"What's wrong with Miami?" I asked her. "What if I want to take in a Marlins game or something?"

"Have a nice time," she said.

"Come on, I'll buy you dinner."

"What? They don't have an Arby's in Deerfield Beach?"

"You know, Martie, I used to wish I could say witty things. Now I just wish that you could."

She started to giggle, "Okay, wise guy. What's in Miami?"

"Cynthia Sinclair."

"Emma's Daughter?" asked Martie.

"That's right."

"I thought you said you brought her back."

"She ran away again," I told her.

"No sweat off your ass, is it? Did Emma ask you to go back and get her?"

"No, she didn't. She knows it wouldn't do any good. She'd just run away again. McCord's probably got a job lined up by now."

"McCord?" asked Martie.

"The gym teacher."

"Oh, that's right. Man, that's creepy," she said.

"Different strokes," I said.

"That's not even funny, Mack. I guess I'm just a little old fashioned."

"I am, too, to tell you the truth," I told her. "But Emma's money spends just as well as ladies with straight daughters."

"It seems dirty, Mack."

"It probably is, but not because of anything Cynthia did. She's just a kid. Her old man made the money, so he's the root of the evil."

"What's his story," asked Martie.

"He started in contraband. First it was bootlegging and then he supposedly became legitimate in the fifties by lending money to people who couldn't afford to pay it back."

"How charming," said Martie. "Foreclosing loans on hardship cases is a surefire way to make a lot of friends."

"Mrs. Sinclair claims that his lack of morality is the reason she left him."

"Sounds like you don't buy it," she said.

"Let's just say I got a different impression from Cynthia."

"In what way?"

I was reluctant to tell Martie that Cynthia alluded to her mother being a hypocrite in that she wasn't the only member of the family who enjoyed the intimate company of both sexes. I figured Martie had been creeped out enough for one day so I just said, "Nothing I can put my finger on. It's just that there's always two sides to every story."

"So why do you want to talk to Cynthia now?" she asked.

"To find out who stole the Picasso."

"Oh, naturally. Why didn't I think of that?"

"Because you don't think like a crook," I told her.

"You make it sound like a character flaw."

"No, it's not a flaw. It's just a handicap."

Chapter Eight

We took I-95 to the South Beach section of Miami and checked into the same hotel where I had found Cynthia and Misty McCord before. I didn't get a peek at the guest register, but I knew that they were there. They wanted to throw the whole hypocritical circumstance in Emma Sinclair's face.

Just as we reached our room, Joey Berio came around a corner and seized my wrist before I could turn the key.

"I'm glad I ran into you, Mr. Willis," he said.

"Joey, what a coincidence." I managed to say in an even tone. "You're staying in the same hotel."

"I'm not staying here, Mr. Willis. I came here looking for you," said Joey. "Your secretary said I could find you here."

"Well, I'll be sure to remember to thank her for that." I was starting to perspire rather heavily. "You certainly found me," I said. "What's up?" I asked not really wanting to know the answer. I wasn't quite sure if he was goofing on me or I was goofing on him.

"Mr. Dimiccia has instructed me to give you a token of his appreciation," he said holding out an envelope in front of him.

"I've done nothing to deserve it, Joey, but thank you anyway," I told him. I noticed Martie was getting a little anxious. She opened her purse and appeared to be reaching inside for a key. I got her eye contact and shook my head no very slightly, hoping that *"The Ice Pick"'* hadn't noticed. The last thing I wanted was any kind of confrontation. For every goomba you shoot, there are two more that come back right behind them.

"Mr. Dimiccia has instructed me to give you this envelope, Mr. Willis. He said if I come back with it, then it better contain a new set of balls because I'm going to need them," said Joey. He looked at Martie and said, "No disrespect, lady."

"No problem, Joey," she said. *"Mack, I think we need to talk."*

"Look, Joey. I haven't done anything to earn the money," I told him. "I'd like to take it, but then I would be beholden to your boss, right? I'm sure you understand. Just tell Mr. Dimiccia that I don't want to get involved, okay?"

"I'll leave it right here," he said. "Right outside your room. You can tell Mr. Dimiccia that we never talked, but I'm not getting back in the car with the envelope, get it?"

"Yeah, I get it, Joey. Have a nice day," I said.

"You too, Mr. Willis." He looked at Martie and said, "Nice ta' meet you, lady." Martie has that effect on everybody.

"A real pleasure . . . *Joey*," she said.

I knew she was going to lay into me any minute, so I said, "Look, Martie, I'll explain everything later. Right now we have to go down to the pool to look for Cynthia."

"What are you going to do with the envelope?" she asked.

"Believe me, Martie, we can't afford to touch it."

"What the fuck are you talking about?" she asked furiously.

"I said I'll explain everything, don't worry."

"It better be good, Willis," she said hotly.

We stopped by the manager's office and told him about the envelope in front of our room.

"It's not yours?" he asked.

"It's not mine," I said honestly.

"You say it's full of cash?" he asked.

"Bursting with cash," I told him.

"Well, aren't *you* the Good Samaritan," he said.

"I'm sure someone will call to claim it. What was your name?" I asked him.

"My name is Vinny Rocca. I own this place."

"It's very nice," I said.

"You live in Miami?" he asked.

"Deerfield Beach."

"You don't remember me, do you?" he asked. "You're Mack, the conga guy, right?"

"Small world," I said checking for Martie's reaction. She was looking at some post cards in a rack. I didn't think she was paying any attention to us.

"Sure, we met before. My bartender hired you guys to play here one night. Remember, I told you that Mayor Angelo Rocca is my brother. That's his Lexus out front."

"That's right, I do remember," I told him.

"You guys still together?"

"I'm afraid not."

"Too bad," he said. "*You were fly*, as they say."

"That's nice of you to say," I told him.

"My wife thought your name was kind of crude, though. '*Painful Bur. . .*'"

"Well, we've got to take off, Vinny. Nice to see you again."

"You, too, Mack. Drop by anytime."

~

Ahh, saved by the job! I grabbed Martie by the arm and led her out the manager's office.

"Let's look down by the pool. I think there's a tiki bar where we can get a beer." I said looking back over my shoulder.

"What's gotten into you, Mack?" she asked. "You're acting really creepy."

"It's called scared, Martie. I just didn't expect to run into that goon back there."

"You're in some kind of trouble, aren't you?"

"Not yet. Look, you just have to trust me, okay? Everything will be fine."

"Nice of you to drag me into it," she said.

"Oh, relax, would you?"

"*You* relax."

~

We found Cynthia and Misty working on their tans down at the pool. I wasn't looking forward to telling Cynthia that her mother wasn't the one looking for her this time and that I was. As I had expected her shoulders drooped slightly and she just said, "It figures."

She was a good kid. All she wanted was a little attention, and I found myself feeling sorry for her. But I was on a case so I had to press on before Cynthia or Misty decided that they didn't have to talk to me if they didn't feel like it. I figured it would be best to tread lightly.

I began, "You know your mother cares about you, Cynthia. She's just having a little trouble letting go. She knows you have a mind of your own and doesn't see the point of me forcing you to go back to Palm Beach."

"What are you doing here?" she asked. "You and your girlfriend just on vacation or something?" She made a point of checking out Martie. *All of Martie,* if you know what I mean. Her friend Misty lifted her sunglasses and sat up in the lounge chair as if suddenly on guard. I guess it's a jungle out there no matter which team you play for. I told her, "No, I'm here on a case. This is my friend Martie Coleman who was nice enough to tag along."

"Pleased to meet you," said Cynthia. She looked very uncomfortable as she said, "Of course, you know Misty."

"Hi, Misty," I offered somewhat awkwardly as well.

"Always a pleasure, Mr. Willis," said the gym teacher dryly.

I said to myself, *Man! This isn't going very well,* and I felt I was just about to lose them when Martie said, "God, I wish I could tan like that. I think I have too much Irish blood or something." She sat down in the lounge chair next to Misty and took off her shirt. Her skin was very white compared to the other two women. She looked at Misty and asked, "Don't you ever worry about getting too much exposure?"

"Not in South Beach," said Cynthia alluding to the clothing optional section of the beach. The two of them startled to giggle. Cynthia asked me, "What's this case you're working on, Mr. Willis? What brings you here if it isn't to drag me back to Palm Beach?"

I sat down on the lounge next to Cynthia and said, "Actually, I'm working for your mother again."

"What does she want, pictures this time?"

"It has nothing to do with you and Ms. McCord, Cynthia. She's hired me to try to recover a stolen painting."

"I don't have it," she said dryly taking a sip of her beer.

"Of course, you don't. I just wanted to ask you if you have any idea who would steal a painting that's too hot to handle."

"Which one was it?" she asked.

"The Old Guitar Player."

"Damn her," said Cynthia. I could see the disappointment in her eyes. I knew she was heartbroken by the loss and that she had nothing to do with the theft. I had to see her face to be sure. That's why I drove to Miami.

"Damn who?" I asked.

"Both of them, the greedy assholes," she said furiously. "I'm beginning to think that my mother is not only a hypocrite, but a sociopath as well."

"Whoa, now," I told her. "Those are pretty strong words to say about your own mother."

"Oh, you know she's guilty. She's just hiring you for show. She wants the insurance money *and* the painting."

She said out loud exactly what I had been thinking all along. I just needed someone to confirm that my cynicism hadn't gone out of control.

"Did someone break into the house?" she asked.

"The painting was on loan to the museum."

"You see? That seals it. My aunt has been trying to get her to release some of her paintings for years. She's always refused her. My mother was never the type to share her position of good fortune. If she finally agreed, she must be up to something."

"Your aunt works at the museum, doesn't she?"

"My aunt is on the board of the gallery and art school."

"She also works in the gift shop, doesn't she?" I asked. "Your aunt is Mrs. Bell."

"That's right. She's a sweetheart, but I can't say the same for her shithead of a daughter, Sarabell."

"Sarabell?" I asked incredulously.

"Well, actually, her name is Sarah. Sarah Bell. I've just always called her Sarabell since we were kids. She's enrolled at the school. Did you know that?" asked Cynthia.

"No, as a matter of fact, I didn't," I told her. I found it very interesting that I had talked to Mrs. Bell about the students at the school, and she failed to mention that her daughter was one of them. Naturally, I asked, "Just what kind of relationship does your mother have with Sarah?"

"Sarah's her niece, of course."

"But do they get along well?" I had to ask.

"They're as close as stink on a turd," said Cynthia.

~

The case was starting to shape up nicely, and speaking of nice shapes, we agreed to tag along with the two sun worshipers to the beach across the street. Naturally, they shed their clothes and insisted that we do the same. That was a mistake. I'm not a prude or anything, and I'd been to nude beaches before, but due to Cynthia's underage status and her relationship with Misty, I felt kind of creepy. The one up side to the situation was that I got to get a look at Martie's body in broad daylight. I don't mind telling you, it was worth it

Even through we cut our walk short after I'd learned how to get in touch with Sarah Bell, there was an unexpected down-side to our excursion. Martie got a really painful sunburn in some very sensitive places. The things we have to endure in the interest of justice. Oh, well, it's a nasty job, but someone has to do it.

Martie was a really good sport about the whole situation, and she didn't even get upset when she noticed Misty checking her out. Cynthia did, and I got the impression that she's a lot more   fragile than the persona she portends to project.

She gave us some good info on Sarah, and I had the feeling that it was only a matter of time before we could zero in on the location of the painting. I was still convinced that it never left the building on Olive Street.

~

We went back to our room at the hotel to take a nap and get cleaned up to go out to dinner. Miami has so many good restaurants that we figured, why waste the trip? Both of us were really wiped out by our little excursion on the beach. To tell the truth, it was really from drinking beer in the middle of the day. We were out as soon as our heads hit the pillows.

We woke up about 6:00 P.M. and took turns showering off all the sweat, salt and sunscreen. After we got dressed, we could still feel the heat radiating off of our bodies. It's amazing how strong the sun is in Florida, even in October.

Dinner was great. We ended up going to this famous steakhouse called Joe's. I was so full that I talked Martie into spending the night at the hotel. I gave Martie the bed, and I tried to sleep on this fold-out couch that had a metal bar right under the middle of the mattress. I gave up after about an hour and then just laid the couch cushions on the floor. Believe it or not, I think it helped my shoulder.

On the way to the car in the hotel parking lot, a large, dark sedan pulled in and came to a stop right in front of us. I assumed that someone important was getting dropped off. I was wrong. The shiny black rear window came down to reveal Sophia Dimiccia's father, sitting there in all his glory. It must have been sixty degrees in that car, but Frankie DeLucca paused to wipe the sweat off his brow before he spoke to me.

I stopped dead in my tracks, knowing it would be useless to try to avoid him and Martie said, "What's going on, Mack?" without really moving her lips.

"Nothing," I said. "Just be still."

"*You* be still," she said. "You're shaking like a leaf."

"Mr. Willis," began DeLucca, "My daughter Sophia hired you to do a job for her. I am respectfully asking you to finish it."

"I don't have what she wants, Mr. DeLucca," I lied. "I'm not even in that line of work anymore." I turned around and started walking toward my car.

Frank DeLucca stopped me with his huge voice when he said, "I'm not finished talking to you yet, Mr. Willis."

I turned around and briefly put my hand on the rear fender of Mayor Rocca's Lexus, which was parked next to my Porsche.

"I'm sorry, Mr. DeLucca. I meant no disrespect. I just don't see how I can help your daughter," I said shakily.

"Let me ask you, what line of business are you in now?" he asked wiping his brow again.

I thought about my job for Emma Sinclair, and I *might* have glanced at the Mayor's car, just briefly, as I said, "I deliver things."

"So you're a pizza boy, eh?" he asked mockingly.

"Not exactly," I said.

Frank DeLucca rolled his window back up, and I watched his fat face disappear behind the piece of shiny, black glass.

Suddenly, both of the sedan's passenger doors burst open and two large men came forth with baseball bats. They immediately started breaking the windows of the Mayor's Lexus. I looked on in horror as they also bashed in the fenders, the trunk lid and the front hood."

"Please don't do that," I said weakly. It made no impression on them.

I further pleaded, "Stop, you're making a mistake," but they just wouldn't listen to me. They continued around the car – breaking every headlight, taillight, tag-light and turn signal. When it was all over, Frank DeLucca's window rolled slowly down again, and he was laughing, "Too bad, pizza boy. I guess you're out of a job." His window rolled back up as they sped away out of the parking lot.

Martie walked slowly up to me with her mouth open and her head cocked slightly to one side. I'll never forget her words biting into me, "Mack Willis. That was the cruelest thing I have ever seen in my life."

"Hey, what can I say? I love my car."

On the way back to Deerfield Beach I filled Martie in on the whole situation with Sophia Dimiccia and her husband, Carmen. I told her that the goon named Joey, (I left out the *ice pick* stuff), worked for Carmen and that Frank DeLucca was Sophia's father.

Frank hated Carmen because he beats Sophia, but Carmen claims that she just likes rough sex.

I told her about the threat to Susan that Carmen was very clear about and that Susan doesn't understand and calls me a coward for not helping Sophia.

"So do you still have the photographs?" asked Martie.

"Yes."

"Send them."

"But Susan. . ."

"Send them, Mack, but not to Sophia. Send them to Frank DeLucca."

"What about Carmen and Giovanni, *The Ice Pick*?"

"Look. If you'd just leveled with Susan in the first place, I'm sure she would have told you to do just that."

"I don't know," I told her.

"Why don't you call her and ask her?"

"All right, I will."

Later that day, I put in a call to Sarah Bell's apartment. I got her machine, but decided not to leave a message. I thought it would be interesting to get Sarah's reaction to my theory in person that the painting was still at the school. Naturally, I expected it to facilitate a panic response - resulting in some kind of incriminating behavior on her part. I was wrong. Sarah turned out to be one cool cookie.

Martie and I drove up to Palm Beach to drop in on Sarah Bell unannounced. Her apartment was called the Surf Club, but the only surf you were likely to find was in the pool. It was located about three blocks in from the beach and had clearly seen better days.

There were iron stains from the sprinkler system on all the sections of stucco on the ground floor, which was surprising, because the lawn looked like it hadn't seen a drop of water in quite a while. Most of the cars in the parking lot were older, including the one that was parked right outside Sarah's apartment.

Sarah met us at the door in a purple string bikini and a black silk sarong wrapped around her waist. I have to admit that I was somewhat taken in by her looks. She was beautiful. Her long, flowing auburn hair and chestnut brown eyes were framed behind a rose tinted blush to her high cheekbones and radiant complexion.

She made Cynthia Sinclair and Misty McCord look like Miss Piggy and Raggedy Ann. No wonder Cynthia hated her. She had beauty *and* talent, assuming she wasn't wasting her time at the art school.

"Excuse my appearance," she said. "I just got in from the beach. Can I get you something to drink?"

"No thanks," I said. "I'm fine."

"How about you?" she asked Martie.

"I'd like a glass of water," Martie said, "but I can get it if you'd like."

"Sure," said Sarah. "The glasses are over the sink and there's ice in the fridge."

Martie went into the kitchen and Sarah said, "My aunt told me that she hired you, Mr. Willis. Do you think you can find it?"

"I'm working on it," I said. "We just got back from Miami where we talked to your cousin Cynthia."

"You don't think that she had anything to do with it, do you?"

"No, of course, not. Cynthia's a good kid. I just wanted to ask her if she knew of any suspicious characters where her mother was concerned."

"Is she still with that gym teacher?" asked Sarah.

"I told Cynthia that I believe that the painting is still in the school."

"What makes you say that?" she asked.

"According to everybody I've talked to, no one had any motive or opportunity to steal it. The school was closed when it disappeared, and yet there was never a break in. Doesn't that sound strange to you?"

"Yes, it does." She fiddled with her sarong and for a moment I thought it was coming untied. I certainly was.

Martie came back in the room and held the glass of ice water to her forehead, "Whew," she said. "This is one hot state you've got here, Mack."

"I'm sorry," said Sarah. "My air conditioning doesn't work."

"Hey, if you can't stand the heat, get out of the South," I told her. "So, Sarah," I continued, "Do you have any ideas?"

She cinched up her sarong a little tighter and said, "Not a one, but I appreciate you trying to help."

"No problem," I said. "That's what I'm here for. I guess we'll head on back to the school and look for something we missed. Thanks for your help, Ms. Bell."

"You're welcome," she said, "but I didn't do anything."

"Oh, every little bit helps," I told her.

"Thanks for the drink," said Martie. "See ya'."

~

When we got back in the car I asked Martie what she learned from the kitchen.

"What do you mean?" she asked.

"I knew you really didn't want a glass of water. You wanted to check out her kitchen – see what kind of tastes she has – what kind of housekeeper she is. Any expensive things that looked out of place?" I asked anxiously.

"Mack, I was thirsty. I wanted a glass of water."

"Oh."

~

I have to admit that Sarah Bell was a pretty cool cutie. She actually had me doubting her involvement until Martie brought me back to terra firma. It was Martie who had the foresight to ask Misty for her cell phone number.

After all, once Misty knew that we weren't interested in interrupting her pedophile love affair, she was more than willing to discreetly pass her number along to a potential date. Martie played along beautifully, which allowed us to keep in contact with the two women in Miami.

She also had the presence of mind to call Misty back to ask the one question, which nailed the reason Sarah was certainly involved in Emma's insurance scam. She was poor.

True, Sarah's mother was on the board at the art school and at The Norton Art Museum, but it was a volunteer position that provided neither a salary nor any form of a discount for member progeny. In other words, Mrs. Bell had a very good reason to work at the gallery gift shop; she needed the money.

Martie learned from Cynthia that Emma was footing the bill for Sarah's rather expensive education. Cynthia loved spilling the beans where her beautiful cousin was concerned.

While Sarah's bloodline enjoyed the good fortune of good looks and talent, her own family merely enjoyed the good fortune of having a fortune. It was a situation that many young girls would exchange in a heartbeat, so naturally, she envied her. Cynthia's lack of maturity prevented her from moving on with her life past the silly names and resentment of Sarah's relationship with her mother. She struck out at Sarah with the only weapon that she had in her pitiable power. She hated her.

Martie and I could only feel sorry for Cynthia. It wasn't our job to aid in her self-actualization. That was the ball dropped by Emma Sinclair long ago. It was sad to watch an impressionable young girl immersed in a damaging relationship, which mistook sex for any kind of genuine emotion. I always find it sad to watch the damage that money can do. Misty was there for the money. Cynthia was there for the lie.

Chapter Nine

The next morning I put in a call to the museum to ask Mrs. Bell why she didn't mention the fact that her daughter, Sarah, attended the gallery art school. She wasn't in. I didn't really suspect her of anything, but I found it kind of odd that she was sort of steering me away from her daughter, if only by omission. Perhaps she had doubts of her own.

I called Susan to tell her that I'd be mailing her a check for twenty-five hundred dollars as soon as Emma Sinclair's check cleared in my account. I owed her roughly twice that much in back salary and alimony, but Susan was never the greedy type. She didn't leave me for more money, she left for more *sanity*.

I also told her that I intended to send the photographs to Frank DeLucca and that she might consider moving into my guest room until the whole thing blows over.

"Are you and Martie sleeping together?" she asked me.

"No," I said honestly. "What business is it of yours?"

"I could care less," she said.

"Then why did you ask?"

"I just didn't want to put myself in a situation to . . . hear it, that's all."

"We sleep in separate rooms, okay?"

"I told you I don't care," she said.

"I'm glad."

"You'd like to sleep with her, wouldn't you?"

"Look, do you want me to send the pictures or not?"

"Of course, I want you to send them. You should have done it about two months ago."

"Then I want you to stay with me for a while, okay?"

"Yes, sir," she said sarcastically.

"You know where the key is. Help yourself."

"Thanks, Mack."

"You're welcome."

Emma Sinclair answered on the fourth ring, "Well, Mr. Willis, what have you found out so far?"

"Not very much, I'm afraid."

"You've had your two days. Please send me the balance of the check I advanced to you. I believe it's eighty-five hundred dollars, correct?"

All of a sudden she was a wizard at finance and seemed to want me out of the picture if you'll pardon the pun. I told her, "I didn't say I've given up, Mrs. Sinclair. In fact, I'm working on a lead that may bare some fruit, so to speak." I had to catch myself from chuckling at Martie's facial expression. She seemed to think I was referring to Sarah Bell as a fruit. Who knows, maybe I was.

"Nonsense, Mr. Willis. You said yourself that after two days the chances of recovery are substantially reduced."

"The leads may be getting colder, but they're not dead," I told her.

"Well, the point is moot as far as I'm concerned. I've already contacted the insurance company and made a claim. If they wish to hire you, then so be it. But as far as you being in my employ - the well has just run dry."

"I'll send the balance of your check, Mrs. Sinclair." There was nothing more to say.

"Thank you, Mr. Willis. Goodnight."

Martie got the gist of the situation by hearing my half of the conversation. She said sourly, "That went well."

"She made no bones about telling me to bug off."

"She called you off a little quickly, don't you think? It doesn't cost her anything unless you succeed, right?"

"Maybe she has more to gain if I fail," I said.

"Especially if you can prove that she's in on it."

"Man, I'd love to burn her, but I don't see how," I said.

"Speaking of burn, my nipples are killing me," said Martie.

"Would you like me to . . .?"

"Never mind!" she said.

I figured I'd better drop the subject so I said, "I can't prove that her niece stole the painting for her, and I can't very well search her house, can I?"

"You know what would be cool?" asked Martie with her eyes lighting up.

"What's that?" I asked.

"If we could get Cynthia to help us steal the painting after Emma collects the insurance money; she couldn't even report it missing."

"I think that falls under the heading of contributing to the corruption of a minor, Martie."

"I know, but I can dream, can't I?"

"It is a good idea, though," I told her. "With any luck, maybe Cynthia will think of it on her own."

"So did you enjoy seeing me without my clothes?" asked Martie.

"Of course, I did."

"Well, I hope it was worth it," she said pulling her tee shirt away from her chest.

"It was to me."

Chapter Ten

When I got Mason on the line he told me that, indeed, Victor was there in New Jersey, and had asked him to produce another section of the glass wire. Mason was optimistic despite the fact that he had abandoned the project about three weeks earlier. He knew that Mike was still burning a glass product with a germanium cladding. It would be a simple matter to configure a section with a fluorine core, but they would have to steal the lab time. No one was authorizing any centrifuge time for doping glass. However, he assured us that he and Mike could somehow work out the details. His mood was intoxicating. He understood the implication of Victor's request.

Victor promised to let us know when he could determine the position of the massive asteroid by the effect that it had on distant celestial bodies. While not actually being able to see it from the observatory, Victor could determine its position by the trail of its gravitational field. When he looked for the changes expected by the asteroid's influence, they weren't there. It had moved!

Victor explained to Mason that any number of celestial events could change the direction of the asteroid. A collision with another large asteroid could move a distant planet into its path. Or an actual supernova many parsecs away could alter its path and not be detectable to the perspective of earthbound observations until it did something that it wasn't supposed to do. For instance, not show up at a specified place and time.

There was no guarantee that we, as a species, were in the clear; however, it was certainly worth another look, or listen, as the case could more accurately be described. The dark matter would be broadcasting an entirely different series of vectors and mass values than the first time that Victor Reese received and interpreted them. They were, of course, intended to forewarn planets that happened to be in harm's dispassionate way. The trick was to utilize the wire on the mountain, once again, to determine if we actually had a future after all.

As fate would have it, Martie and I were, once again, concerned with Victor Reese's safety. Although Bill Riley and Scott Palmer, also known as Uri, were killed in a failed attempt to intercept Victor in the Atlantic City Airport rental-car-return parking lot, Martie and I were well aware that another bothersome, although almost comical, personality named Dimitri was still somewhere at large in New Jersey. No one had witnessed any violence where Dimitri was concerned; however, we urged Victor to contact Martie's office and obtain an armed escort. Martie was able to assemble it from my home in Florida. I was impressed.

When she got off the phone, she crossed her arms in front of her chest and began to shake uncontrollably. I went to her, concerned and put my arms around her, "My God, Martie. What's the matter?" I asked her. She couldn't even speak. I was beginning to get really worried about her when she said, "I want it, Mack," still shaking. I was more confused than ever and asked her, "You want what, Martie?"

"I want my life," she said as her shoulders began to quake.

"Of course, you want your life. What kind of thing is that to say?" I asked her.

"You don't understand, Mack. I want it now because it was taken away from me." She was crying hard. Her once formidable and tough exterior was now shattered.

"Hey, take it easy, honey. Calm down. You're safe here."

"Yeah, we're safe," she cried. "For how long?"

"I'm not following you."

"I can't go on like this!" she screamed. "I thought I could, but I can't. If that makes me a weakling, then tough shit," she bellowed through her tears.

"Nobody's a weakling, Martie. Nobody's keeping score. Get it?"

"What does it matter? We're just waiting, and we're helpless."

"I'll tell you what it matters. I love you."

"What?"

"I said, I love you."

She wiped away her tears with the palms of her hands and said, "Aw shit, Willis! And now you're going soft on me." We both started to laugh, and then I said, "I'm serious, Martie. I *do* love you."

"Good job, Mack. Give me something to live for now that it's too late," she started crying again. "Jesus, what's wrong with me?" she said. Her shoulders started quaking again. "When we first found out from Victor that we were all toast, I figured, '*Oh, well, what the hell. It was nice while it lasted. Let's party.*' But now I know I was just hiding my true feelings. I felt robbed, God damn it. And now. . ." she sobbed again and caught her breath, "now that it was taken away . . . and now that we might get it back. . . I want to live. I want to live now more than I ever did. Hell, Mack, I think I might even love you too."

"That's so romantic," I teased.

"Shut up," she said, starting to cry again. "God, I can't remember ever being so embarrassed. Look at me."

"You look beautiful," I told her truthfully.

"I look awful," she said.

"You look absolutely naked. I can see into your soul, Martie, and it's never looked more beautiful."

"Whew!" she said wiping away more tears. "That's a lot to get off my chest." Martie walked over to the couch and sat down. She held her head in her hands, and I noticed that she was rocking back and forth ever so slightly.

"How do you feel?" I asked her.

"I'll let you know as soon as I can catch my breath," she said, "*and* when we hear from Victor again."

"I know what you mean. I'd like to hold Victor's hand all the way back to Hawaii. I hope he doesn't somehow blow it," I told her. I felt as helpless as she did, but I knew that if I was any kind of friend to her that I should appear to be strong. As usual, she beat me to the punch.

"He'll be fine," she said. "I guess *we'll* be fine, as well."

"You sound a lot better."

"I'm all right. You want to go to bed?" she asked me.

"Sure," I said. "Maybe even sleep." I got her to smile.

Chapter Eleven

I had changed also. That is to say I had a change in attitude once I learned that there may be a chance our destiny had taken a decidedly better turn in terms of longevity. I found myself feeling more than a little bit ashamed of my behavior regarding Cynthia Sinclair. When I thought that we were all going to be blown to cosmic dust, the prospect of a nice kid being corrupted by a homosexual, opportunistic gym teacher didn't amount to much in the whole scheme of things.

Now that I thought that we all might have something to look forward to, I decided to sing an entirely different tune. Regardless of Victor's findings, I was determined to make a difference in the life of that screwed up little kid.

My first order of business was to place a call to Sarah Bell's apartment in Palm Beach, Florida. I decided to play a hunch and got right to the chase, "I know how you did it, Sarah," I told her.

"Excuse me?" she asked. "Know how I did what?"

"Oh, that's right," I continued. "I suppose I should say I know how you intend to do it because the painting hasn't actually left the building yet, has it?"

"I don't know what you're talking about," she said.

"Oh, yes, you do," I gambled. "Your aunt needed you to steal the painting from the art school, and here's how you planned to do it."

"I'm hanging up the phone, Mr. Willis."

"It was the staples, Sarah. That's how you made your mistake," I lied. I can be devious as hell when I want to be. I continued on with my fabrication, "When I examined the room where all the students were working on their copies of The Old Guitar Player, I noticed three small staples on the floor. You must have overlooked them when you were sweeping the floor. I know the students act as custodians, so you must have chosen a day when it was your turn to clean the studio "

"You're crazy, Mr. Willis. I'm not going to listen to another word. . ."

"I noticed when I was talking to your mother that all the canvasses in the supply store are prefabricated rather neatly and come already stapled to their frames. So why the loose staples, I asked myself?"

"I'm sure I have no idea," said Sarah.

"Because someone stapled a copy of The Old Guitar Player over the original painting. It's a simple matter to take home your own work, isn't it, Sarah?" I asked her. She was dead silent on the other end of the line, so I continued, "You had all the time in the world to make a copy of the painting with a slightly enlarged white border at your aunt's home. Then you removed it from the frame and rolled it up into a tight tube you could sneak into the gallery under a long skirt." There was still no response from Sarah, so I knew I could move in for the kill. "Then you had only to staple the copy you made over the original and destroy the copy you had been working on in class. Your aunt's plan was very simple, wasn't it?

"True, it must have been uncomfortable for you walking out of the gallery with the broken wooden frame down the small of your back. All in all, I'm sure it was a small price to pay for a quality education. You would have gotten away with it if it weren't for the staples." I waited patiently on the line. Experience had taught me that in a pregnant moment such as that, the first one who talks usually loses. I was right.

"What do you plan to do?" she asked finally.

"I intend to strike a deal with your aunt. You probably won't do any time," I said, although I knew that she wouldn't. "I've written a letter to the insurance company describing how you attempted to defraud them and made a copy for the Palm Beach police chief. Call your aunt and tell her that I'm on my way over to talk business."

"You plan to blackmail her, is that it?" she asked hopefully.

"I'd prefer to call it a finder's fee. After all, your aunt did retain my services to do just that."

"I'll call her," said Sarah.

"I knew you would."

Chapter Twelve

Martie Coleman was actually impressed by my little deduction and what turned out to be my subsequent deception. She accompanied me to Emma Sinclair's house but decided to wait in the car for me. She didn't want to be a witness to anything that might come back to haunt her. It was a shame she missed the look on Emma's face. Her complexion was absolutely scarlet as she wrote out the check. I left with a signed confession - just in case she decided to go ahead with the plan to charge the insurance company and claim that I extorted her. Some kindly old ladies are just not to be trusted. When I got back in the car, Martie asked me, "Did you get your ten grand?"

When I handed Martie the check she got very quiet for a while. It wasn't until we tuned south on I-95 when she said, "You didn't actually blackmail her did you?"

"Nope."

"Forty-five thousand dollars? What's it for?" she asked.

"As it turns out, I'm still working for the old girl in a sense."

"What's that supposed to mean?" she asked clearly confused.

"I've got one more duty to perform. Something I should have done a while ago. I just forgot who I was for a while."

"Mack Willis. Just what the hell are you talking about?"

"Listen and learn," I said. I turned on my cell phone and placed a long distance call from West Palm to Miami. I put it on the speaker-phone so Martie could listen in, "Misty, it's Mack Willis. You alone?"

"Yeah, Cynthia's down at the pool. What can I do for you, Mack?" she asked.

"I'm glad you asked that, Misty. You see, I've been kind of bored lately, and I've decided that I need a hobby."

"What kind of a hobby?" she asked guardedly.

"Well, actually, you're it."

"Pardon me?" she asked.

"You're my new hobby, Misty. I've decided that from now on, it's my job to make your life a living hell. Sound like fun?"

"What are you talking about, Mack?" she asked.

"I'm talking about the delinquency of a minor, lewd and lascivious behavior, pedophilia, any of that ring a bell?"

"Why the sudden turn around?"

"Let's just say I found God."

"Just my luck," she said sourly.

"It's not all bad news, Misty. I'm about to make you a deal you can't refuse."

"So now you're the Godfather, is that it?"

"I'll tell you who I am. I'm your worst nightmare. I'm a guy who turned his back on a criminal act for money. I did it because I had reason to believe that none of this mattered, but I was wrong. That was my job, being wrong. Now I've got a new job, *being right*. Now that I want to look myself in the mirror again, I have a lot to repent for, and I'm starting with you. You want to hear the deal?"

"I'm listening," she said.

"Smart girl. You can either do a lot of jail time, and I'm talking hard time, guaranteed, or you can walk away from Cynthia with a cashier's check for thirty thousand dollars. What do you say?"

"Emma's money?" she asked.

"Emma's money," I told her. "I'm authorized to leave the check in an envelope that you'll have to sign for at the Palm Beach Post Office. Right after you drop off Cynthia at her mother's house and tell her that you're taking the deal."

"What's to stop me from cashing the check and then going back for Cynthia?" she asked.

"I'll tell you. You don't really give a rat's ass for Cynthia. All you wanted was the money in the first place, so take it and run. Either that or you know I'll find you and make the charges stick. What's it gonna' be, Misty? Would you like to retain your freedom with a check for thirty grand, or do I send you a soap on a rope?"

"You're a first class bastard, Willis."

"I know, but I'm getting better. What do I tell Mrs. Sinclair? Does she have a deal or not?"

"I don't have much choice."

"No, you don't." I broke the connection.

Martie said, "Nicely done. Do you think she'll take the deal?"

"She'll take it," I said.

"You know, if you stick with it, you might make a fine P.I. after all," said Martie.

"I just earned twelve grand for making a phone call," I had to boast.

"I'm the one who got you the phone number," she reminded me.

"I'll cut you in for twenty percent," I offered.

"You're getting off cheap."

"No I'm not," I told her. "Susan gets most of *my* share."

~

About a week later I got a telephone call from Frank DeLucca. He told me that his daughter Sophia was in the hospital with a bruised trachea. He also told me that I wouldn't be hearing from Carmen Dimiccia or Giovanni Berio anymore. I didn't ask him why he knew that, but I believed every word of it. I still look over my shoulder from time to time for Joey. Something that he said about *"beyond the grave."* What a character. Speaking of characters, Frank DeLucca turned out to be a nice guy after all. He was a pretty good sport about the whole car thing. The first thing he said to me was, "You know, Mayor Rocca was a friend of mine. *Was,* is the operative word in that sentence, Mr. Willis. But the car was insured, so I guess there's no real harm done. I'm willing to forget the whole incident because you finally did the right thing."

"I'm very glad to hear that," I told him.

"My little Sophia admitted to me that the whole rough sex thing was her idea, but after she ended up in the hospital, her husband decided to go away for a while. A long while, so you probably won't be seeing him any time soon."

"What about his pal, Joey Berio?" I asked.

"Uh, he decided to go with him."

Epilogue

As you probably have discerned by the fact that we're all still here, the Reese-Spender asteroid had been moved to a harmless orbit through our solar system. I have to admit that when we finally got the phone call from Victor, a tear escaped from my eye. It was a small tear. P.I.'s don't really cry; we all know that. I managed to quickly wipe it away before Martie noticed a thing.

She bawled like a baby. The hard-nosed government agent who had saved my life in a New Jersey firefight had been reduced to an emotional disaster area. I loved that side of her. I loved her for showing it to me.

I never really counted on having a female partner for my investigations, but I have to admit I could have done a whole lot worse. I managed to convince Martie to quit the Department of Defense despite the huge loss of benefits. One of my strongest arguments was, *"What good is a health insurance policy when you're dead?"*

On a slightly more serious note and tone of voice, I asked Martie to marry me. She accepted, sort of, but we haven't even talked about setting a date. Believe it or not, that was over three years ago. I think we're both inclined to take a nice long test drive of our relationship.

I'm trying to become a better person. I don't dig up any dirt for ugly divorces anymore. Martie and I mostly work for the insurance companies. You'd be surprised to learn how many expensive items are highly insured, then stolen, and somehow miraculously turn up in the most unlikely places when we're on the job. You see? I *said* it helps to think like a criminal.

Oh, by the way, Cynthia Sinclair is now in college and has a nice boyfriend. They plan to get married after they graduate.

Emma Sinclair was relieved by the discovery of The Old Guitar Player, which was carelessly misplaced at the school. Coincidentally, it was her niece, Sarah, who made the discovery. Naturally, Emma cancelled her claim to the insurance company.

Sarah now teaches art history and composition at the Norton. I told you she was good.

As far as dark matter is concerned, there's a whole new Mack Willis who looks up at the night sky. I owe an awful lot to dark matter. It took away something very dear to me, for a short while, and then gave it back when I learned not to take it for granted. I suppose, in some small way, it's also responsible for bringing Martie Coleman and me together.

Dark matter showed me that although we're destined to remain very alone as a planet, we're no more insignificant than any other one. We're important enough to shower with a constant vigil of protection. We are well cared for, whether or not we choose to heed the warnings. It's not unlike a parent trying to protect a helpless child by saying, "Careful, honey, the stove is hot."

Indeed, it is *hot* out there. And it's *dark* out there. But if you listen very carefully, you'll discover that *it isn't really all that quiet.*

Part Three

Fore The

Love

Of

Money

Chapter One

"Y ou're a good person, Eddie," said Sharon Mitchell.

"I am now," said Eddie Juneau, "because of you."

"You've always been good, except you had just lost your way for a little while. Now, that's ancient history - remember that."

"You make it sound so easy, Sharon. You know it's not."

"I know. I also know I believe in you."

"I love you Sharon. If I were a woman, I'd ask you to marry me."

"If you were a woman, I'd probably say yes."

"Any time you want to try on a male for size..."

"You'll be the first to know," she told him.

"I know you're lying, but thanks. I have so much to thank you for. You saved my life, you know that?"

"You saved your own life, Eddie. I was just lucky enough to witness it."

"I owe you so much," he said. "I feel ashamed that the band won't play your fund raiser. You know I'll play for free any time you need me."

"I know, Eddie, don't worry about it. Maybe Wayne's father will sponsor you guys. But even if he doesn't, I just want to thank you for trying."

"I'd do anything for you and The Second Wind."

"Here's the house," she said turning into the driveway and past the huge iron gates. "Did you say Wayne was going to be here? I haven't seen him for months now."

"Did he beat it?" asked Eddie.

"Beat what," asked Sharon.

"Oxycontin."

"I'm not sure anyone does, Eddie"

"God, I hate that stuff."

"Because you're a good person."

"For now..."

"Hush, I don't want to hear any of that. Too many people are counting on you."

"That's what bothers me," said Eddie. "It's not just me anymore."

"That's the secret, Eddie. You have to ask more of yourself than just caring for yourself. Do you understand?"

"Not really."

"Well, you will. Trust me."

As they drove up to the large Tudor style house, Sharon Mitchell made note of all the cars parked around the long circular driveway with the ornate fountain in the center. "It looks like they're having a party. We might want to come back later."

"This might work to our advantage," said Eddie. "He'll probably want to get rid of us before anyone knows where we're coming from."

"You might want to rethink your approach."

"Look, Sharon. Wayne Jr. is a good guy, but he's a junkie. You saved his life, whether or not you want to take credit for it. I know he quit the program, but he wouldn't have made it if you didn't force him into The Second Wind. Now, if his hoity-toity daddy isn't appreciative or wants to just shove the whole business under the rug, let him tell us so in person."

"Make sure you offer him the anonymous patron package. He'll still get the write off and won't have to be associated with the clinic."

"Oh, I'm sure that's what he'll go for. He's building some megabuck homes on the old golf course property."

"That's so sad," said Sharon. "My dad taught me to play there."

"That's progress," said Eddie.

"I wonder," she said. "Maybe some things are better left untouched."

Sharon parked her Jetta behind a line of large SUV's. Eddie noticed that the Lincoln Navigator at the very front of the line had a license plate which had the numeral, "*1*" with a much smaller number next to it.

"Egotist," he said. "That's Wayne Jr.'s ride. What the hell does he mean by *1*? All I can think of is, *1 SORRY BASS PLAYER*."

"Easy, boy. Remember why we're here," she told him.

As they neared the front door, they could hear voices and music coming from the back yard. Thinking that no one might hear the doorbell, they decided to peek through the gate at the side of the house and see if they could get Mr. Markham's attention. Sharon led the way, and when she opened the latch the first thing she said was, "Oh, dear. Eddie, I think we've made a terrible mistake."

A low, gravely voice just inside the gate was all too eager to agree with that very sentiment, "Mr. Markham's little get together is by invitation only, Miss," said the voice as a large handgun appeared and was waved in their direction.

"We're sorry," said Sharon. "We'll be leaving now. Don't bother Mr. Markham."

"Not so fast," said the graveled voice. "You would be smart to follow me," he said as he came out through the gate toward the front of the house and led Sharon and Eddie back to the front door. "Walk this way," he said opening the front door. Eddie had the impulse to just grab Sharon and make a break for her car. As it turns out, it would have been the only move that could have saved their lives.

But Eddie didn't see what Sharon did as she peeked through the gate to the backyard. Much more importantly, he didn't see who Sharon had recognized sitting there with Wayne Markham, Sr., enjoying the sexual gesticulations of a bevy of scantily clad young women. Unfortunately for Sharon and Eddie, it wasn't what was happening in the back yard, it was who was there. Tony Giancarlo was a notorious drug kingpin living in the Miami area who had recently appeared several times in the news. He was currently *"at large"* with an arrest warrant hanging over his head, which would return him to his native New York City and an imminent conviction with a sentence of at least ten years in prison.

The man with the gravely voice led Sharon and Eddie to a sitting room inside of Wayne Markham's house. "Wait here," he said and left the room.

"What's going on?" said Eddie. "What's the big deal?"

"I think that we're in a lot of trouble, Eddie."

"What kind of trouble?" asked Eddie.

"The kind you don't get out of," she said miserably.

~

The life of a private investigator is a lot less exciting than most of us have been led to believe. I suppose television shows are to blame for that. But no one would want to watch a show about my life, so I guess I can forgive the writers for embellishing the truth. My name is Mackenzie *"Mack"* Willis, and I live in a sleepy little Florida community called Deerfield Beach.

As the name implies, there is a beach, but there aren't any deer. Maybe there were at one time or another, but it wouldn't be the first time the animals were crowded out by the real estate developers in Florida. Guaranteed, if you go to a place called Manatee Cove or Indian Harbour, you won't find any manatees or Indians.

What you will find are people who feel they have the right to squeeze every ounce of potential value out of a place and then move on. People do strange things for money, which brings me to the point in question about two bodies found lying on the fourteenth green at Shoreline Pines Golf Course.

Shoreline Pines is a quiet little course just north of Deerfield Beach and south of Boca Raton. You could find it just past the Hillsboro Lighthouse if you were looking, but why would you? The course has been out of business for about six months now. Why, you might ask, does a nice, little golf course on the Atlantic Ocean go out of business? Naturally, the answer is money.

The sins of Shoreline Pines were that it was just too small and just too damned nice. I know that sounds like a contradiction, but being a "*nice place*" is a sure way to get horribly exploited in Florida. Nice, historically stands in the way of progress and prosperity. Remember the unwritten code of the snowbird: "*Do unto others and then move south and do it unto them.*"

There were actually pines on the course, right along the ocean, just like Naples on the Gulf Coast used to have. They were there in all their glory until about five months ago when the bulldozers came in. It took them about thirty minutes to destroy what Mother Nature chose to devote half a century to.

There were beautifully majestic live oaks adorned with Spanish moss, but they had to go also unless they had the courtesy to grow near the perimeter of the lots once they were subdivided. For the most part, they just didn't fit in with the design plans of the Mediterranean style villas. They were to be called, "*Francisco's Landing,*" or some such nonsense. The only thing that ever landed there was a golf ball when someone sliced it off the third tee. Being a golfer, I knew the course pretty well; in fact, it used to be one of my favorites. I'm not very long off the tee and neither was Shoreline Pines.

It was a beautiful little *executive course,* meaning it wasn't nearly as long as a traditional layout. Par was only sixty, because it had a dozen par-three's and only six par-four's. The longer courses in the area always got the lion's share of play, so they decided that a golf course was not the best possible use of prime oceanfront property. I guess, in my heart, I knew it was only a matter of time.

Up in Brevard County, about one-hundred-twenty miles North, there are two nice executive courses on the beachside. Their names are Aquarina and Spessard Holland, which is an Arnold Palmer design in honor of the great Florida Statesman and one time Governor. Those architects had the foresight to build their courses *across the street from the ocean.* A man with any vision of the future would have known that the silly dream called Shoreline Pines was doomed from the start. But Francisco's Landing isn't landing anytime soon either. They've put a stop-job on the whole operation due to the bodies that were found on the fourteenth green. That's where I come in. The chief of the Deerfield Beach Police Department is a man named Peter Wells, and he knows when to call in the services of a good P.I. To be perfectly honest, I got the job because I used to work for Peter in his homicide section until I got the ax. He didn't want to fire me, but the other homicide detective was his wife, Mildred, so when they decided that Deerfield Beach only needed one of us, I was the one to go.

After the work on Francisco's Landing had been halted, the developers insisted that an independent investigation should be conducted concurrently with that of the local police department. The bottom line is that nobody trusted anybody, and in the interest of progress, the whole mess should be tied up nice and neatly and filed away as soon as possible. Never mind the fact that two people are dead.

One of the benefits of working as a private investigator is the people you meet. I mentioned that my life is relatively uneventful, but some of the lives of the people I meet are unbelievable. One such person is my lovely fiancée, Martie Coleman. She's a tall, shapely blond who used to work for the Department of Defense. Every morning I wake up and look at her sleeping form next to me, and I have to resist the impulse to pinch myself. She's that beautiful. We met in New Jersey when I was doing a temporary gig with a band called *Blue Cactus*.

Aside from performing discreet investigations, I also play the congas rather well, if I do say so myself. Either job earns roughly the same amount of money, which is to say that, I won't be purchasing a residence in Francisco's Landing anytime soon.

Martie's work for the Department of Defense was as a real spy. I'd never met a spy before, so you can imagine my delight when I discovered she had me *in her sights*. I also learned that before her Defense Department position, her job was with the D.E.A. Can you believe it? She was a real spy who used to bust drug dealers, and she likes to hang out with me. Life is good sometimes. I get to sort-of live vicariously through her. She's done all the cool things that I'd dreamt of doing when I first had the idea of going into private investigations.

Now she helps me with my caseload, and she cooks pretty well to boot. I told you life was good. Well, life is almost good. Actually, she was ticked off when I agreed to take the case for Peter Wells. It's all because we were supposed to be heading off to an island in the Bahamas called Long Island. I had promised to take her bone fishing with this really good guide I know named Wellington Taylor. We'd both been feeling a little burned out lately, and I promised her that we could take some time off for a little R & R.

Martie likes to kind of *mother me* sometimes, but she'd never admit it. I know if she heard me say that that she'd say I'm full of crap, but it's the truth. I've got the kind of personality that women just can't resist bossing around. It's a rare and precious personality trait, I assure you. On a good day, I can turn a Palestinian suicide bomber into a Jewish mother.

Martie insisted on coming with me to talk to Peter at the station. We got in my little blue Porsche and tried to be nice to each other on the way downtown.

"Why don't you ever listen to anyone, Mack?"

I should say, *I* tried to be nice on the way downtown. Martie was acting kind of rough as usual. She rarely ever gives me a break. I told her, "I do listen, all the time."

"You only hear what you want to. Susan was right about you, you'll never change."

"What do you mean?" I asked her. "What did she say?" Susan is my ex-wife and present secretary and unfortunately had recently been trading stories about me with Martie. Most of them are untrue, I can assure you.

"Susan said you have selective hearing."

"That sounds like a very nice quality," I told her.

"It means that you ignore people most of the time, Mack." We were driving by the old sold out golf course at the time, and I was curious to see that the sales trailer was buzzing with perspective buyers by the look of the parking lot. Francisco's landing was really starting to catch on.

I had the distinct impression that Martie had asked me something, but I couldn't remember what it was. I said in the most polite tone that I owned, "I'm sorry, honey, what were you saying?"

"Forget it," she said icily. She seemed a little miffed. I couldn't have forgotten our anniversary because we weren't even married.

"Come on, Martie. What were you saying? I was just distracted by the scene of the crime over there," I said motioning toward the golf course with my head.

"I was saying that you don't seem to take people seriously sometimes."

"No, you weren't. You were saying that I ignore people."

"Are you trying to deliberately piss me off?" she asked. I realized the irony of the situation and started to laugh. I could see her face turning red as she said, "Well, I'm glad you think you're funny."

"No, it's not that," I told her still laughing. "Sometimes I sort of record what people are saying in my head and then play it back a short time later. You see, I'm actually listening very closely, but I get distracted easily. It's not that I don't give a shit, I really do. I hear every word you say; it's just that I have A.D.D. or something."

"I'm sorry," she said. "What were you saying, dear? I wasn't listening."

"I said I love you, Martie."

"I love you too, Mack," she said. "I'm just not sure why."

Chapter Two

Pete Wells is a pretty nice guy for the most part. I almost miss working for him, but I don't miss working with Mildred. She's a nice enough lady, I suppose, but she was always so determined to prove herself to her husband that on more than one occasion she stuck us right in the middle of harm's way. She would think nothing of barging into an abandoned apartment in the middle of "crack town" and demanding answers to some pretty direct questions. I found myself walking out of the room backwards, thanking them for not turning us into completely ventilated human beings. I was hoping that she was still faring well, but I didn't exactly know how to pose the question. Finally, after I introduced Martie to Pete, I barged ahead and let the question fly, "How's Mildred?" I asked hoping for some surprisingly good news. I got it.

"She's good. She retired from the department," he said. *Thank God*, I didn't say, but Martie noticed my trepidation and actually asked, "Mack, are you feeling all right?"

"I'm fine," I told her firmly. "Let's continue, shall we?"

"Hey, lighten up, Mack," said Peter. "John and Jane aren't going anywhere," he said. I resented his tone. By John and Jane, he meant that the victims found at the golf course haven't been identified yet. Just because he hadn't attached a name to them didn't give him the right to make jokes about them.

It brought back the memory that Mildred wasn't the only reason I was glad to have left the Deerfield Beach Police Department.

I know he didn't really mean any harm, but I had read in the newspaper that the two bodies found on the golf course were in their early twenties. It's such a shame to be cut short of your life before you have the time to make some really bad decisions like marrying your secretary.

I'm sorry. I haven't been myself lately. Maybe Martie was right, and we should have gone bone fishing. I got right down to business, "I read that they were kids."

"Yeah, early twenties," said Peter. "Looks like drugs."

"You're kidding?" I asked him. "Both of them?"

"Needle marks, puke at the scene," then he caught himself, "I'm sorry, Ms. Coleman."

"Don't worry about Martie," I told him. "She's been around the block. D.E.A. and Defense."

"Really?" asked Peter. "I'm impressed, Mack. You've found a woman who doesn't mind you bringing your work home."

I wondered just what the hell he meant by that comment, but decided to let it go. *Did Susan talk to Mildred, too?* I wondered. You know what they say: *Just because you're paranoid doesn't mean that they're not out to get you.*

"Whose puke?" asked Martie.

"Well, I'm not sure, but usually when someone shoots heroin into their bloodstream the first thing they do is throw up, that is *if* there's anything in their stomach," said Peter. His tone of voice was sort of condescending, and I could see Martie's talons were about to come out.

"Look, Mr. Wells, Mack just told you that I was once with the D.E.A. Are you trying to suggest that I just never paid attention to my work? I'd be willing to bet that I know a hell of a lot more about junkies than you do."

Peter was caught off guard, "I'm sorry, Ms. Coleman. I didn't mean to be a smart ass."

"Forget it," said Martie. "I just meant to say that the vomit could tell you a few things. One, who got sick; two, what they ate; and three, if it's from a third person and therefore a possible murderer."

"Yes, I know. We've thought of that, but we don't have the financial resources to order DNA tests without something more to go on. Right now we've just got two kids who decided to get high on the fourteenth green and got carried away."

"Maybe carried away is the operative phrase," I said.

"What? You mean that they were dumped? As of now we've got nothing that points to that."

"No tire tracks?" I asked.

"Not at the scene," he said. "There're a bunch of tracks on other parts of the course because the kids party there almost every night."

"You mean they go four-wheeling?" asked Martie.

"Hell, no," said Peter. "They use the God damn golf carts."

"You've got to be kidding," I said.

"I wish I was. We have to send a car out there all the time. The little bastards broke into the cart barn and charged up about a dozen carts before we caught hold of them."

"Who calls you?" I asked.

"There's still a night watchman, but he can't be everywhere at once. For the most part, I think he just gives up."

"Can't say that I blame him," said Martie. "It must be very frustrating for him."

"It isn't still Ben Maddox?" I asked him.

"The one and only," he said.

"Well, I'll be damned. He worked there when I was a kid. He always wanted to be a greens-keeper, but never went to school as far as I know."

"Probably didn't," said Peter. "He went from maintenance to night watchman after he had a heart attack."

"If I remember correctly, he was a club-maker, wasn't he?"

"That's right. He set up a little shop inside the cart barn. Mostly, he just did grip jobs for people he knew, but for re-shafting they usually went to a pro."

"He carry a gun?" I asked.

"He carries his old putter and uses it like a cane. He says all he needs is a cell phone and a bottle of whiskey," he said.

"Have you gotten his statement?" I asked.

"I haven't forgotten how to do my job, Mack."

"He obviously didn't see anything then."

"His trailer is by the clubhouse. The fourteenth green, as you know, is over by the beach on the north side. Then there's the four home holes along the ocean back to the clubhouse. That's got to be about a quarter mile away."

"Almost," I told him. I knew exactly how far it was. They were my favorite four holes in golf. Fifteen was a hundred-forty yards from the tips. Sixteen was a par four, about three-twenty. Seventeen was another par four about four-hundred, and eighteen was the prettiest little par three in all of Broward County. It measured about one-seventy.   That's a total of one thousand and thirty yards of beautiful oceanfront golf that unfortunately is now just a memory. I've had it in the back of my mind to grab a seven iron and sneak on myself for a few quick holes during twilight.   Hell, I knew Ben Maddox pretty well from the old days. He probably wouldn't even kick me off.

I was wondering if Martie would like to learn the game when Peter said, "There's not much to go on, Mack. We're running the prints, and their pictures are going to run in tomorrow's paper." He was ushering us out of his office.

"Before I leave, Pete, maybe you should tell me who we're working for."

"His name is Wayne Markham. He's the one developing the property and calling it Francisco's Landing. The county sold him the course to generate capital, plus a lot of tax revenue."

"How much money are we talking about, Pete?"

"About twenty million bucks near as I can tell."

"You still play cards with the Mayor?" I asked him.

"Yeah, what about it?"

"Then I guess you know exactly what the number is, don't you?"

"I guess some things never change, Mack."

"Only the names to protect the innocent," I told him.

Chapter Three

We left the station and drove directly to Shoreline Pines. The sales office was set up in the old clubhouse and was still open, so we pretended we were in the market for a townhouse and walked right in. A pretty, young sales associate approached us right away and shook both of our hands, "Welcome to Francisco's Landing," she said.

"Thank you, Ms. Cooper," I said getting her name from her ID badge.

"It's Mrs. Cooper, but you can call me Ann."

"Thank you, Ann. My name is Mack Willis, and my lovely friend here is Martie Coleman."

"Nice to meet you, Martie," said Ann.

"Which of you is interested in purchasing a home here in Francisco's Landing?" she asked.

"Both of us," said Martie. "We're planning on living in sin."

Ann Cooper never missed a beat when she replied, "Oh, that's too bad. I was hoping to sell a townhouse to each of you."

"That's a little more room than we need right now, but maybe later," I said laughing. Martie didn't think it was so funny, but it got a smile out of Ann.

"Are you looking for direct oceanfront?" she asked.

"How many are left?" I asked avoiding her effort to direct the conversation.

"A few," she said. "Most of the north and south end lots are taken, but we still have about six left in the center of the community.

They're very nice lots, half-acre, and near the clubhouse and tennis courts.

"What is the asking price?" I asked.

"Actually, we don't actually have asking prices per se here at Francisco's Landing. We take closed bidding above the set minimum for each lot."

"What is the minimum bid?" I asked her. She was starting to bug me. Any minute I was going to lay back and let her have to deal with Martie. That would show her.

"The minimum for an interior direct oceanfront lot is six-hundred-fifty thousand," she said icily.

"How much was the minimum bid on the north and south ends?" I asked.

"They are no longer available," she said.

"I know, but how much did they go for?" I asked pointedly.

"That information is confidential, Mr. Willis," she said. I was impressed that she remembered my name.

"Oh, I know," I said with mock urgency. "We wouldn't want to let out any classified information, would we? At least not until next month when they close on the lots and any six-year-old can get the exact figure off of his computer. You're aware that the tax rolls are public information, aren't you, Ann?" I asked her pointedly.

"Look, Mr. Willis. I'm not trying to be difficult, but I've been asked not to discuss previous bids because it might interfere with the ones currently being considered. Honestly, it's not my idea. You'll just have to wait until they close, and then you can look them up yourself."

"I'm sorry, Ann," I told her. "I'm not trying to be a jerk,

either. It's just that I'm trying to get a handle on just how much money the whole park might generate for Mr. Wayne Markham."

"You're a P.I., aren't you?"

"Yes, I am."

"I think you'd better leave," she said.

"Can I have a map of the park?" I asked hopefully. "Maybe with some prices written on the lots?"

"Please leave, Mr. Willis. I'm trying to do my job, and we're very busy."

"Take it easy, Ann," said Martie. "We're going. Come on, Mack. I'm not sure that I want to live on an interior lot. I'm sure those north and south guys will think that they own the place." That's why it's so much fun hanging out with Martie. What can you say to a beautiful woman who can put you down so effortlessly? I usually just say *let's go to bed.*

When we left the sales office, Martie said she wanted to go to lunch, but I wanted to seek out old man Maddox. I told her that I had a few questions for him, but the truth was, I wanted to ask his permission to walk the place with a seven iron. After all, I wasn't going to interrupt any work going on. The police had closed down all operations until the investigation was concluded.

Martie got her wish. I knocked on Maddox's trailer, but there was no answer. She took me to this health food place she had discovered. My sandwich was okay, but I got a bunch of sprouts stuck in my teeth.

Chapter Four

I called Peter's office and asked if he wouldn't mind faxing me a layout of the proposed community. He was more than happy to cooperate. After all, the quicker I could come to a conclusion the better. Then all he had to do was concur with my deduction and then the Mayor and Markham would be off his back. Twenty million was a joke. There had to be at least twenty lots on the ocean alone. Add to that the forty or so interior lakefront lots and it adds up to a lot more than twenty million. *But why hide it? It'll all be public record soon. What was Peter's angle?* I wondered. I was getting the impression that he was a silent partner. I didn't think that he would look the other way for money, but then again I guess people can change. I hoped not if for no other reason than for Mildred's sake.

I also asked Peter if they had any more leads as to the identity of the victims. He said no, but that he would keep me posted. For some reason I didn't believe him. He had no reason to lie about anything as far as I could see. I was convinced that I had to see farther. I drove Martie home so she could take a nap, and I drove over to the morgue to talk to the coroner. His name was Jim Bailey, and I had met him a number of times before when I worked with Mildred in homicide. He had just finished the autopsies on the two victims found at the golf course. I continued to refer to them as victims because I just wasn't buying the idea that they went to the golf course to get high. Kids drink beer at night on the golf course, but I don't think it's their favorite place to shoot smack. People don't like wide-open spaces when they're getting high. Furthermore, why shoot it in the first place. Most of the guitar players that I know who use it like to smoke it. It's called *chasing the dragon* for some reason that I'm not quite sure of. I'll have to ask Martie what she knows about the way kids use heroin these days. If they smoke it, then why did the kids on the golf course have needle marks?

The next day, the local paper got the hits they were looking for. Six different people called in and identified the male victim from the artist's sketch placed in the paper. There was still no word on the identity of the female, but at least now we had a place to start. It turns out that the male was the lead guitarist in a local club band called Rancid Salmon. They were a *grunge* group mixed with a little bit of trance-like *Ska*. It's mostly just loud screaming to a bunch of out-of-tune guitars. They were playing in a club called The Cavern in Ft. Lauderdale. I convinced Martie to go with me that night to talk to some of the band members.

Just as I had suspected, the band hadn't missed a beat - at least as far as finding someone to fill in for the late guitarist. His name was Eddie Juneau, which I took to refer to where he came from rather than his actual last name. Naturally, I asked the waif of a lead singer named, Boo Baby, "Was Eddie from Alaska?"

"Don't know. Why do you ask?"

"Juneau is the name of a city there."

"Could be."

"Did you like him?"

"He was okay," she said. "The new guy is better."

"You think he really OD'd?" I asked.

"How should I know?"

"You use smack?" I asked her.

"Sometimes," she said. "You're a P.I., right? Not a cop?"

"I'm not a cop." I motioned to Martie on the dance-floor and said, "Neither is she."

"Yeah, we get high. It helps us get in the mood for Ska."

"Do you smoke it or shoot it?"

"I usually keester it," she said.

"I'm sorry," I said. "I don't understand."

"I stick it up my ass."

"Honestly?"

"Don't knock it if you've never tried it."

"What about Eddie? Did he like to shoot it?"

"No, way, man. He smoked it in a crack pipe."

"Are you sure he didn't use needles?" I asked.

"No, I'm not sure. Sorry." She turned around and walked away toward the rest of the band. Her body language told me she was done talking, and I could tell that the other band members were not going to give me the time of day. I wondered if they would have cared if they knew I suspected foul play. Probably not. I walked over and asked her one more question, "Hey, Boo Baby, did Eddie have a girl?"

"Don't know," she said.

"Anybody else know?" I asked them collectively.

"Nope."

Chapter Five

We were driving back to Deerfield along the beach by way of Lauderdale by the Sea. It's a nice little stretch of A1A where you can actually see the Atlantic Ocean from time to time between the hotels, restaurants and condominiums. The Cavern had really done a number on Martie. The first thing she said when we got in the car was, "I feel like I need a shower. God, those people are worthless. My hair smells like pot smoke."

"Tell me about it," I said shaking my head. I'd been around drug users before, but those people were scumbags. "By the way, you could have warned me about keestering," I said. Martie started to laugh.

"Who told you about it?" she asked. "The skinny bitch?"

"Yeah, what's up with that?"

"It's just another way to get off. Like shooting between your toes. An addict will do anything to get well if they're sick."

"Sick? You mean like withdrawal," I asked.

"That's right"

"But what's the point of keestering?" I had to ask.

"It's all about blood vessels, Mack. Wherever the mucus membranes are the thinnest they can interface effectively."

"Come again?"

"What happens when someone snorts coke?"

"They get high."

"That's right, but do you know why?"

"Because the coke gets absorbed into the bloodstream."

"Through the mucus membrane, right?"

"I guess so."

"It's the same with the colon. There's a very thin mucus membrane that allows the drug to enter the bloodstream."

"Jesus, that's sick."

"Of course, it's sick. It's a disease, Mack. That's why they call it an addiction."

"Yeah, well, you could have warned me, that's all. I felt like I was a hundred years old back there."

"You were. We both were. I'm kind of glad that I don't have to grow up in this world, Mack."

"I hear ya'."

~

There was a harvest moon rising out of the sea when we reached Deerfield Beach, so we decided to walk down by the waters edge. "Very romantic, Mack," said Martie.

"It is with the right person." I kissed her forehead. I'm glad I resisted the notion of rolling around in the surf like Burt Lancaster in *From Here to Eternity*. I'm as romantic as the next guy, but thank God I have my limits. I wanted to just enjoy the moment with her. When you work with your life-partner, sometimes you have to work at not bringing the job home. I wanted to talk about the case, and she could sense it. She let me off the hook by saying, "Tell it."

I pretended that I didn't know what she was talking about, "You're beautiful, that's what."

"What do you want to ask me about the case?" she asked.

"Why were there needle marks on the bodies?"

"Because maybe they were junkies?" she said sarcastically.

"Maybe they were, but the girl at the club said that Eddie wasn't into needles."

"You're thinking it's a homicide," she said.

"That's right. Do you disagree?" I asked her.

"I don't have an opinion. I'm just keeping you honest."

"It looks like bullshit and you know it. Two kids OD at the same time, at the same place, and a good cop like Peter Wells wants to shove it all under the rug. It stinks."

"I didn't get that impression from Peter," she said.

"You don't know him like I do. He's a bulldog. At least he used to be one. He never believed in coincidences. Ten years ago he would be fighting to get answers instead of making light comments about how the corpses aren't going anywhere. Either he's really changed, or else he's in someone else's pocket."

"You'd better be sure, before you accuse him of anything like that, Mack. You haven't been shot for about three years, if I remember correctly. You wouldn't want to ruin a nice healthy streak like that, would you?"

"I've got you to watch my back, babe."

"I don't carry a weapon anymore, Mack."

"Maybe you should start," I told her half seriously.

"Maybe you should start. What's wrong with you, you're licensed?"

"You're a better shot," I told her.

"Then practice for God's sake."

Chapter Six

The next day I called Peter and asked him if he had anything new on the female victim.

"Casualty, Mack. She's a casualty in the war against drugs. It's a war we're losing by the way."

"That's a nice speech, Pete. Save it for the junior high school students."

"Just what is your problem, Mack? Jesus, I don't know you anymore."

"That's right you don't, Peter. But I'm not the one who's changed, *you* are."

"Okay, I'll bite. How have I changed?"

"The old Pete would have said, 'tough shit, Willis,' but you've just invited me to keep talking. You want to know just how much I know. That's pretty scary, Peter."

"Mack, you're trying to manufacture a case where there isn't one," said Peter. He sounded a lot like the old partner that I rode a squad car with twelve years ago. I wanted to believe him.

"What's going on, Pete? I mean what's *really* going on?" I asked him.

"I'll tell you," he said. "I've got a really rich guy trying to develop this fancy-shmancy tract of townhouses. Two kids wind up dead on the property, so naturally it's my job to get to the bottom of it. After all, I am the fucking Chief of Police for God's sake. But will they let me do my job? Will they trust me to do my job? Hell, no! They insist on an independent investigation - like I don't know my ass from a hole in the ground. That's when I called you. That's what's *really* going on, okay?"

"You called me because you know me well enough to push me around, is that it?" I challenged. "Imagine how I feel. You called me, and then you act like I've got no business sticking my nose in your business. How would you feel, man?"

"I don't know, Mack. All I know is that I'm feeling pressure from two sides, and you're the only one I can bitch at, so you've just been elected whipping boy."

"Lucky me," I said sarcastically.

"Lucky you," he said and then broke the connection.

My feelings were really mixed up at that point. I wanted to just curl up in bed with Martie and tell the whole bunch of them to fuck off. Then there was a side of me who kept looking for my old friend, Peter. I was looking for someone who watched my back once upon a time and trusted me to look after his all-too-fearless wife, Mildred. I wanted to know I could count on his friendship. I knew at that very moment that I *needed* friends. I knew that I'd let myself drift away from everybody who mattered in my life except Martie. She was feeling the strain, I could tell. I don't know why these things happen, but I didn't want to be an island. I wanted to have a poker group again. I wanted to join a bowling league. I wanted to be Mack Willis again or else reinvent myself as a conga player and go on the college concert tour. But Martie meant so much to me. I was really confused at that point.

I found myself actually praying that I was wrong about Peter. Maybe he was just telling it like he saw it. Maybe there was nothing else to it. Maybe I was getting paranoid about a conspiracy that really didn't exist, but I didn't think so. Being the Rhodes Scholar that I am, I got drunk. I got really drunk. I started drinking and playing an acoustic guitar until I couldn't play anymore. I'm kind of anal about my music, so I won't play it when I start to suck. I'll quit before I ever misrepresent my babies. That's how I think about my music. You see, I write all the songs that I play. I used to do cover tunes. In fact, a few years back I did a gig with my brother-in-law's band, *Blue Cactus*, in New Jersey. That's where I met Martie.

But I've already mentioned that, haven't I? I'm sorry. I'm just not myself lately. God, I need some time off. I promised Martie we could go bonefishing, but . . . the ringing phone took me out of my reverie,

"Mack! We got it." It was Peter.

"Peter?"

"Listen, we've ID'd the girl found on the golf course with Eddie. Her name was Sharon Mitchell, and she was a really good kid. She wasn't a drug user at all; in fact, I'll bet she'd never done a drug in her whole life."

"I knew it. Well, I actually didn't know it, but I just didn't have a good feeling about the whole thing."

"I know, Mack. I owe you an apology."

"No, you don't, Pete."

"Yes, I do, so let me do it for God's sake."

"Okay, man. We need to catch up."

"Yes, we do. Let me tell you something. I've been under a little, no, maybe more than a little pressure from Mayor Bennet to get the Shoreline Pines thing tied up quickly. He's Markham's partner in the whole thing."

"You could have told me, Pete."

"Look, I said I was sorry. I didn't think there was anything going on until I learned the identity of the girl. I'm sorry, but the guy was a throw away. He threw his life away a long time ago, but the girl was a diamond in the rough."

"What are you saying, Pete? Could you please spell it out for me?"

"She was a counselor, Mack. A *drug counselor.* She never did a drug in her young life. She lost her brother to an overdose and it devastated her. She walked on water, for God's sake."

"Jesus."

"I'm sure she's there with him now. She worked at a drug abuse rehabilitation house in Pompano. She was what's known as a coat-puller. She got down and dirty with addicts who everybody else gave up on. When a junkie's family gave up on him, she was there to become his new family. There's a list as long as your arm of people who owe their lives to her. In other words, she ain't no throw away, and I'm sorry that you had to call me on the carpet."

"Forget it. What now?" I asked.

"Now I'm moving in on Markham's front lawn. Fuck the Mayor. This is an elected position anyway. He didn't appoint me, and even if he did, I wouldn't lay down for that asshole or any other one."

"I know you wouldn't, Pete. I'm proud to call you my friend, man."

"You too, man. We ought to start up a card group just like the old days. The group I play with now has escalated out of my league if you know what I mean."

"I know," I said. "Give my best to Mildred."

"I will. Listen, when you get a chance, come on down and get the skinny on this girl. I could use your help."

"You got it."

Chapter Seven

When I asked Martie if she wanted to come with me to the station, she declined. She said she wanted to go to the beach and work on her tan. She's really fair skinned, so I knew she was bullshitting me, but I also knew there was a method to her madness. She has a lot of good qualities, and one of them is knowing what someone needs even before they do. She was right about my needing to meet with Pete without her as a distraction. I had a few healing moments in his office. That's not to say that I'm a kind of guy who likes to get *in touch with his feelings* or *seek out his innermost demons* with some kind of primal scream bullshit. I was just glad to have a pal again. It was like getting back something that I didn't even know was missing. Like finding a twenty-dollar bill in your pants pocket after they'd gone through the laundry – maybe even something a whole lot better.

When I got to the stationhouse the mood had changed dramatically. The desk sergeant was a pretty woman named Lois Johnson, whom I hadn't noticed before - the difference being the change in her mood. She was smiling as she noticed me enter the building. "Go right in, Mr. Willis. Chief Wells is expecting you."

"Thank you, Sergeant Johnson," I said noticing her nametag. I walked into Peter's office and found him looking over some paperwork.

"Mack, I'm glad you're here," he said looking up briefly. I'll be with you in a minute. He continued reading for a moment and then said, "This is the profile of the girl. Such a shame," he said shaking his head. "Eddie Juneau was part of her caseload. According to this report, he was clean."

"Really?" I asked. "My, oh, my, the plot thickens."

"Apparently so. I was just about to go back and look at the crime scene. Care to join me?"

"Crime scene?" I asked pointedly.

"It is now," he said. "I said I was sorry."

"Pardon me for rubbing it in. I'm not right very often, so I have to get the mileage out of it when I can."

"You want to ride with me?" he asked.

"Can I work the siren," I asked facetiously.

He shook his head and laughed, "No, you can't."

We arrived at the old golf course at about 3:00 P.M. The sky was kind of overcast, and the wind was whipping up. There was still no sign of Old Ben Maddox, and I became convinced that the best way to find him was to sneak onto the course and play a few holes. Every time I sneaked onto a course in the past, I had gotten caught.

Peter and I parked his cruiser at the clubhouse and walked into the sales office. I found Ann Cooper and told her, "I'm back."

"How nice," she said dryly. The office was nearly empty, so she couldn't claim that I was wasting her time. Peter wasn't in uniform, so I introduced him to her.

"We'd like to borrow one of your golf carts Ms. Cooper," asked Peter.

"It's Mrs. Cooper, Pete, but you can call her Ann."

"That's right," she said turning a little red, "my name is Ann. I've already met Mr. Willis. . ."

"Please, call me Mack."

"As I was saying, I've met Mr. Willis before, when he and a friend tried to misrepresent their intention to purchase a unit here at Francisco's Landing," she said icily.

"Are you aware that a crime has been committed here recently?" asked Peter.

"I was told that it was an. . . accident."

"Yeah, well, that was then, Ann, and this is now," said Pete. "Now we think it was a crime, possibly a murder. Would you like to cooperate with the investigating officer, or would you like to have a pissing contest?"

"I'll get the key," she said.

~

We drove over to the fourteenth green where the patches of rye grass had overtaken the Bermuda. They looked like the hands of a hundred people reaching out of the Earth toward the heavens. It was hard to believe that once I used to scrutinize every minute nuance of the contour that might affect the direction of my ball.

The grain would grow toward the setting sun, so looking west, there would be a sheen that would glisten in the afternoon. You knew you had a relatively fast putt in that direction, especially on the front where it ran downhill. Conversely, from the back left of the green you knew it was against the grain and uphill, which meant that your putt would be much slower, and it wouldn't take the break as much.

It was a strange feeling. Now that the once lovingly manicured section of grass had gone ragged and unruly, I could understand how gravity and the subtle contours would direct the path of my ball when struck from any section of the green. I had never before given it such a thorough examination even when it was such an integral component of trying to make par or birdie on the fourteenth hole. I had birdied the hole many times, but it was usually after a kick-in distance produced by a lucky second shot or else a no-brainer from forty feet. I don't ever remember *reading* the green as intensely as I had when Peter and I drove up there in Ann Cooper's golf cart. I saw every significant aspect *except* the one we had specifically gone there to discover. Martie Coleman was the one to see it when we walked the course the next day.

Peter and I examined the chalk outlines of where the bodies lay and I mentioned that the arms were conspicuously absent. Peter told me that they were folded across their chest as though they were gazing up at the stars and had fallen asleep. I asked him if the sky was clear on the night before the day they were found, and he admitted that he hadn't checked. I told him the point was moot because we knew that the girl had not willingly taken the drug that had stopped her heart.

A further examination of her body had revealed the possible abrasions from a rope used to briefly restrain her. Another curious observation was that the outlines of their feet were very narrow as well. Peter told me that the reason for that was because their feet were crossed when they were found. "So their arms were crossed," I said, "and their feet as well, and they were found lying face up looking into the sky."

"That's right," said Peter. "What?" he asked. "You think they were posed? By the killer?"

"Maybe by someone other than the killer," I suggested.

"But what for?" he asked.

"I don't know. I'm just not seeing it," I had to admit. The last thing that I took notice of was that just beneath both of their feet was the hole. It was the location of the cup where the flag was last placed six months earlier.

"There's something that we're missing, Pete," I told him. "Something just doesn't seem right."

"Two kids have died, Mack. Now we think they were probably killed, that's what's bothering you. It bothers me, too."

"But there's something else," I told him.

"Why don't you sleep on it, buddy? Come on, I could use a drink," said Peter. I guess he was declaring himself officially off-duty.

Chapter Eight

Martie had spent the afternoon cooking. She had grilled some fresh Mahi Mahi with just a touch of blackened seasoning. Then she tossed large chunks of the fish into a Caesar salad and served it with a lobster bisque for an appetizer. As usual, everything was delicious, and it was just what I needed to distract me from the case. We made love and then drifted off into what I hoped would be a wonderfully restful sleep. It wasn't meant to be.

That was the night that Ben Maddox's trailer burned to the ground. We got the call from Peter about 4:00 A.M. We came upon the scene and could immediately see that the trailer had totally melted. The fire marshall said that it probably reached fifteen-hundred degrees in about ten minutes. *God, those things are firetraps,* I thought. Does it look like arson?" I asked him.

"Who are you?" he asked me with irritation clearly in his voice. I figured that the only reason he didn't tell me to bug off was that I was standing next to Martie.

"This is Mack Willis," said Peter to the marshall. "He's a local P.I."

"I know you," he said. "You also play the congas, right?"

"Small world," I said. "What started the fire?" I asked. "Any accelerate presence, like hydrocarbons?"

"None yet. My guess, at this time, is bad wiring or a shorted out heater."

"It's not that cold out," I mentioned.

"Not to you, but you're not a seventy-three year old man like Ben Maddox."

"Was he inside?" I asked fearing the obvious. It had burned in the dead of night.

"God, no," said the marshall. "No sign of any bodies, pets or otherwise."

"Thank God for that," said Martie. Somehow I had the feeling she had spoken too soon. We left Peter and drove back home to get a couple more hours sleep. We woke up around nine, which is later than usual and had coffee and a couple of almond biscotti that Martie had gotten at the Pompano Beach Mall. I persuaded her to walk the old course with me because I figured that with news of the fire, we might run into Ben Maddox. I remember liking the old guy back in the old days, and I wanted to offer him a place to crash until he could get settled. I remembered that he had a niece named Cindy in the area and she used to work at the Coral Springs Hospital out on Sample Road. When I reached Cindy by phone, she told me she had heard about her uncle's trailer fire and was very concerned about him. She claimed that she hadn't heard from him in about a week.

After I cleared it with Pete, I took Martie over to the course to walk the back nine that runs along the ocean. I also wanted to go out and swing a golf club.

I gave Martie a five iron, and I took a seven. She had a pretty good swing for a snowbird. Her golf seasons were about six months throughout the year. Being a resident of Florida meant that I could play golf 365 days a year. We started on ten and worked our way over to fourteen. We had to use the one club for all our shots, which really isn't all that difficult if you're any kind of golfer.

We couldn't reach the par four's in regulation, which is using only two strokes, so we called them par five's. You're allowed to redesign a course when forced to use only one club, especially if the course has been closed down for six months. We reached the fourteenth hole and were both two over par, which isn't too bad considering we had never practiced putting with an iron before. I pointed out the chalk outlines of the victims as soon as we reached the green. Martie commented, "It looks so sad. You can just imagine them lying there."

"It reminds me of another time I saw dead bodies on a golf course," I told her. "I wasn't there in person - I saw them on TV. It was the saddest thing I had ever seen. A pro tournament was being held in Orlando and a fierce thunderstorm just formed out of nowhere. The players fled to the clubhouse, but a lot of the spectators were caught in it. There were about five of them standing underneath a tree when it got hit by lightning. It killed all of them instantly. They just fell over and were lying at the base of the tree like spokes of a wheel. It was horrible." She looked over at the chalk outlines on the green and said, "Not spokes of a wheel, Mack, hands of a clock."

Then it hit me that she was right. I knew that there was something bothering me about the crime scene, but I couldn't put my finger on it. As soon as Martie said it, I could see it clearly. If due North was twelve o'clock, which I assumed that it was, then the bodies were placed at exactly one o'clock.

The male victim was the big hand on the twelve, and the female victim was the little hand on the one. The bodies were placed to show one o'clock on the fourteenth green. I was sure that whoever had arranged the bodies had chosen that particular green. Why bother to pose the victims like the face of a clock unless you are trying to send a message. We were so excited that we ran back to the car so I could call Pete on my cell phone, "Pete, it's Mack."

"Hi, Mack," he said. "Have you checked out the rehab house down in Pompano yet?"

"Not yet, but listen. I think Martie hit on something that we missed. The bodies on the green were placed in a configuration of exactly one o'clock if the green was a clock face with due north being the twelve."

"Jesus, how did we miss that?" he asked.

"Who knows? Anyway, what do you want to bet that the number combination one-fourteen means something?"

"You're probably right. That's good work, Mack. It might be a house number, or possibly a time of day, like, 1:14 A.M. or 1:14 P.M."

"Can you get a look at the phone records of Bennet and Markham?" I asked.

"You bet your ass I can," said Pete. "Go to the half-way house and then meet me back here later this afternoon. If anything comes up that I think you need, I'll call you on your cell."

"Sounds good," I said and then broke the connection. I told Martie, "Pete says atta-boy, Martie. I don't know why I missed that. It was so obvious."

"If you hadn't said the phrase, *'spokes on a wheel,'* I might never have seen it," she said.

"Yes, you would've, but thanks," I told her.

Chapter Nine

The name of the halfway house was The Second Wind Habitat. It was located in Pompano just off of Fourteenth Street on Old Dixie Highway. The grounds were nicely trimmed, and the building looked as if it had just gotten a fresh coat of paint. The whole neighborhood was a lot nicer than I had expected - the only shortfall being that it got unbelievably loud when a train went by.

The director's name was Dr. Judith Myers, and she greeted us warmly and was eager to talk about Sharon Mitchell. "She was like a daughter to me," she said.

"I'm very sorry for your loss," I told her.

"Thank you, Mr. Willis. Everyone here loved Sharon, so it goes without saying that we all are hoping that you can find her killer."

"You're convinced that she was murdered?" I asked even though I knew the answer.

"Oh, definitely," she said. "There's no doubt about it. The police said that there were drugs in her system."

"And Sharon couldn't possibly have used drugs?" asked Martie.

"Not a chance. It just wasn't in her make-up to consider such a thing. It would be like a Muslim going to a Rave, or a Hindu eating a hamburger. It just couldn't happen."

"Did you know the man that was found with her?" I asked. "He went by the name Eddie Juneau," I added.

"Not personally. We get a lot of turnover in a house like this. However, when I heard the name from Chief Wells, I looked in her case files and found him there."

"Are the case files assigned a number," asked Martie.

"Yes, Ms. Coleman. All of them are entered into the house files and numbered accordingly. Then the case worker files the patient's progress notes and therapy credit hours for each day that the case is active."

"Was Eddie Juneau's case still active?" I asked.

"No, he hadn't been with us for about six months. He came to us with a rather severe oxycontin addiction, and we helped him step down with three days of Methadone treatments. As far as I know, he hadn't been back since."

"Was there any chance that Eddie was romantically involved with Sharon Mitchell," asked Martie.

"I hardly think so," she said with certainty. "A man like Eddie was definitely not her type. In fact, *any man was not her type* if you catch my drift."

"Do you know if she had any contact with Eddie since he left The Second Wind Habitat?" I asked.

"I don't see why she would," said Dr. Myers, "unless it had something to do with the fundraiser."

"Fundraiser? For the Habitat?" asked Martie. I could see the wheels turning in her pretty blonde head.

"Yes, The Second Wind Habitat holds a fundraising telethon on Channel Fifty-one, the all-night channel out of Ft. Lauderdale. Sharon routinely recruits some of the entertainers for the telethon."

"Like singers, rock bands, things like that?" I asked.

"That's right," said Dr. Myers.

"Eddie Juneau was in a rock band. Did you know that?"

"No, I didn't," she said.

Martie was on a roll, "Dr. Myers, is it possible that Sharon approached Eddie to get his band to play on the telethon?"

"I suppose so," she said. "But who would want to kill her for that, for God's sake. She was such an angel," I could see tears forming in the doctor's eyes.

"It may not have anything to do with her murder, Dr. Myers," I said. "I'm just trying to connect Eddie to Sharon Mitchell on the night they were killed. Do most of the entertainers donate their performances on the telethon, or do you pay them?"

"Sometimes they perform as a donation, and sometimes they are sponsored by local businesses."

I was wondering just what kind of local business would like to have their name associated with a grunge band called *Rancid Salmon*. Being the sharp P. I. that I am, I ruled out restaurants almost right away. I only had two more questions for the good doctor, Judith Myers. The first one was, "Do you suppose we could get a copy of the names on Sharon Mitchell's case files?"

"I would love to cooperate with you, Mr. Willis, but you aren't a policeman, are you?" she asked hopefully.

"No, I'm not," I told her.

"I'm afraid we have a few confidentiality issues here at the Habitat. I'm sure you understand."

I could see that the conflict of interest was tearing her apart, and then she asked me, "Could you please come back with a policeman, possibly even a warrant, Mr. Willis?"

"I'll see what I can do," I told her. "Just one more question, Dr. Myers. What was Eddie Juneau's case number?"

She looked down at the printout on her desk and said, "The first thing listed is the caseworker's initials. Mr. Juneau's case number was SM-one-eleven. Why? Is that significant in some way?" she asked.

"Not really," I told her. "Thank you for your help."

Chapter Ten

We headed back to Peter's office to tell him what we had learned at The Second Wind Habitat. Peter had run into a dead end with the phone records. We still hadn't found the significance of the number one-fourteen. We were starting to think that there wasn't one. Peter said there wouldn't be a problem getting a warrant for examining Sharon Mitchell's files. Needless to say, we were all anxious to learn the identity of number SM-one-fourteen.

That turned out to be a dead end as well. Case number SM-one-fourteen had died in a car crash four months earlier. I was beginning to think that maybe Eddie killed Sharon Mitchell in some kind of depressed murder-suicide or something. Hey, it happens, believe me. If you read the paper enough, you learn that *everything* happens sooner or later.

Peter was still under pressure from Mayor   Bennet to wrap things up so that he and Markham could get back to the business of getting rich. Ben Maddox's trailer fire had stirred things up briefly, but everyone was starting to cry coincidence again and that Ben was probably off somewhere sleeping off a good binge.

I had to admit to Peter that as certain as I felt about the two kids being killed together by a third party - it looked as if there wasn't very much to go to the D.A. with.   We had to come up with something more concrete in order to keep the case open. As it turned out,   concrete was not the answer, sand was. Sand, as in the green-side bunker of hole number one of Shoreline Pines Golf Club.

As usual, the kids were partying on the course at night, even though they had disabled all of the golf carts in the barn. They mostly just wanted a place to drink beer. One of them made the grizzly discovery of a hand sticking out of the sand by the number one green. It was Ben Maddox. He had been struck on the head with a blunt object. The murder weapon was probably his own putter, which was discovered buried in the sand right along side of him. Ben was trying to blackmail the killer. I was sure of it and so was Peter.

Ben probably had some physical evidence against the killer, or else he never would have contacted him in the first place. I was sure that he thought to hide it in a very secret place, and that was why his entire trailer was burned to the ground. I voiced my suspicions to Ben's niece and told her to be extra cautious in the near future in case Ben had thought to mail her a copy of the evidence.

Peter hit a form of pay dirt when he seized a copy of Sharon Mitchell's files. It turned out that Wayne Markham, Jr., was one of Sharon's cases. He had a serious heroin addiction, and he had stopped visiting The Second Wind Habitat well short of his completed rehabilitation.

According to her notes, when she mentioned that he needed to remove himself from his exposure to heroin he said it was impossible. He said his life was surrounded by drugs and there was nowhere else to go. When Sharon asked Wayne what his father did for a living, he said that he was in the import - export business. She decided not to ask exactly what it was that he imported. She didn't feel that she needed to.

Peter, Martie and I decided to pay an unofficial call on Wayne Markham Sr. Peter told us that we had no evidence to charge Mr.

Markham with any crime. He just wanted to get his response to a couple of questions regarding Sharon Mitchell. Markham met us at the door and led us into a large study just to the left of the foyer. He didn't ask us to sit.

"Good afternoon, Chief Wells. Have you concluded your investigation into the deaths of the two victims at Shoreline Pines?"

"You mean Francisco's Landing, don't you, Mr. Markham?"

"That's right," he said. "That old beater of a golf course is finally dead."

"Just like Ben Maddox," I said.

"And you are?" asked Markham.

"Mack Willis," I said, "and this is Martie Coleman."

"A pleasure," said Markham looking at Martie. She has that effect on everyone.

"I was sorry to hear about Ben Maddox," he said. "It seems that an abandoned golf course is a rather hazardous place. The sooner that it's bulldozed under and the construction gets back on schedule, the better. Wouldn't you agree, Chief?"

"Possibly," said Peter. "Mr. Markham, did you know the female victim, a Miss Sharon Mitchell?"

"No, I didn't. Why?"

"Did you know that she was your son's drug councilor at one time?"

"That's a lie," said Markham hotly.

"It's a matter of record," said Peter.

"Look, all kids get in trouble," said Markham. "That's all behind us now."

"Did Miss Mitchell recently ask you to have your import/export business sponsor an act for a telethon?" asked Peter.

"I've already told you I've never met the woman."

"Yes, you did," continued Peter. "Have you ever heard of the name *Rancid Salmon*?"

"I haven't the slightest idea what you're talking about."

"What instrument does your son play?" I asked him.

"IIc plays the. . ," Markham was starting to look somewhat rattled. "Look, Chief, what's this all about? Should I be talking to my lawyer?"

"I don't know," said Peter. "Do you think you need a lawyer?"

"I haven't committed any crime if that's what you mean?"

"Then why would you need a lawyer?"

"I think we're finished talking here, Chief Wells. I'm not going to say another word until you can arrest me. Obviously you can't, or we wouldn't have been having this conversation in the first place."

"Thank you, Mr. Markham. We'll let ourselves out."

Chapter Eleven

We drove back toward the station in relative silence. Finally, Martie said, "Of course, he's lying."

"Of course," said Peter.

"But we can't prove it," I said.

"That's right, we can't," said Peter.

We kept driving, and I began playing back some of the conversations I had had during the past few days. It's a curious habit that I have - a somewhat bothersome by-product of an eidetic memory. People with photographic memories can memorize things that they see with uncanny detail. An eidetic memory is much less precise; however, it does allow me to replay conversations and music in my head and recapture all of the original inflections and nuances. It can be helpful sometimes, but it also keeps me up at night.

I continued to play back the conversations of the past few days. It seemed like there was something missing that was lying just outside of my conscious mind. Martie broke the silence with, "Maddox should have made a copy of the evidence. If he had he would still be alive. Leaving it in his trailer was a terrible idea," she said.

"Of course, it was!" I nearly screamed.

"What? What is it?" said Peter excitedly.

"It *would* have been a terrible idea to leave the evidence in the trailer or anyplace else for that matter. That's why he didn't. He carried it with him at all times."

"What are you talking about?" asked Martie.

"Of course!" said Peter excitedly. "How could I be so stupid?" "Mack, *now* you get to work the siren."

I turned on the siren and we ran every traffic light back to the stationhouse. We ran inside and Sergeant Johnson asked, "Chief, what's going on?"

"Watch the front door, Lois," said Peter out of breath. He then added, "Please tell me Ben Maddox's putter is still in the evidence room?"

"It's there, but the lab report said there were no prints on it, not even Ben's."

"We're not looking for prints, Lois. We're looking for what's *inside* the putter."

"Inside?" she asked in a confused tone of voice.

"Just watch the door. Nobody gets past you, got it?"

"I got it."

"Good."

The three of us entered the evidence room and locked the door behind us. Peter took the putter, held it up to his ear and rapidly shook it back and fourth.

"He wouldn't have let it shuffle around in there, would he?" I asked hopefully.

"God, I hope you're right," he said.

Peter took a utility knife out of a desk drawer and cut the grip off of the putter. He looked inside. "There's something in there," he said. He went back to the drawer and produced a pair of needle-nosed pliers.

"Bingo." I said when he slid something out of the shaft.

"You've *got* to be kidding?" asked Martie.

"That was the best place to hide it," I told them. "That way he could keep it with him at all times."

"Keep what with him?" she asked.

"This," said Peter producing two photographs and a brief letter rolled up into a tight tube. The first photograph was of a license plate. Although it was grainy and the only light was from the little light bulbs on either side, the number one was clearly visible. Next to the number-one there was also a relatively small number-fourteen.

Wayne Markham Jr. had a vanity plate made for his Lincoln Navigator that had been given to him by his father. Many different people want the number one for their license plate, so the additional number is necessary and is issued on a first-come, first-serve basis.

The second photograph was a shot from some distance away and showed a man lifting a body out of the back of the Navigator. The quality of the photographs was surprisingly good despite being taken in the dim starlight and a waning moon. A brief letter read as follows:

To whom it may concern. If you are reading this letter then, unfortunately, I'm dead. Please tell my niece, Cindy, that I'm sorry for what I tried to do. I was a witness to those poor kids being left on the fourteenth tee by Wayne Markham and some other devil that works for him. The fourteenth is the little par three, only about one-hundred-and ten-yards from the tips, so it wasn't too far to take the bodies to the green.

I took the pictures with the digital camera that Cindy gave me for Christmas last year. Then I enlarged them on my computer and saw the large number one and the small number fourteen on the license plate. They were already on the fourteenth hole, so that's when I got the idea for the clock face. I knew whose car it was. I've known Wayne Junior for years, but I knew he didn't have anything to do with the crime. I recognized his father and the other man the night they dropped off the bodies, so I knew where to send the pictures.

I know that Wayne Markham, Sr., is responsible for the murder of those two poor young kids. As I said before, if you're reading this note, then he is also responsible for my murder. I hope this letter and photographs help you to put him in jail for the rest of his life or even have him executed so he can burn in hell!

Sincerely, Ben Maddox
Senior Greens-keeper (Retired)
Shoreline Pines Golf Course

P.S. I'm sorry I tried to blackmail the bastard, but he put me out of a job, and when I asked him if he could give me another one, he said I was too old, so fuck him!

~

"I couldn't have said it better myself," said Peter.

"How did you guess it was in the putter, Mack?" asked Martie.

"It was something that Peter had said a couple days earlier. He said Old Ben used to re-grip golf clubs as a service for the players at Shoreline Pines. I knew it was child's play for him to pop off his old grip, put the evidence inside the putter and glue on another one. The whole operation probably took him about five minutes, tops."

"Hey, Mack, how would you like your old job back?" said Peter.

"No, thanks, Pete. But thanks for asking," I told him.

Martie gave me a big kiss on the cheek and said, "You get the atta-boy, Mack." I love it when she says that.

Part Four

Heart

Of Stone

Prologue

"**M**ay I help you?" asked the ancient Viennese jeweler.

"My name is Harold Barnes. You left a message at my hotel, The Kensington Palace. Are you Mr. Schulte?"

"Ahh, yes, the American."

"Have you finished?" asked Barnes.

"Oh, it's finished," said the old man.

"How did it turn out?" he asked. "Are you pleased?"

"I can assure you, Mr. Barnes, that the copy I've made for you is every bit the *diamantiferous dropping* of the original."

"Would it take an expert to spot the difference?"

"Don't be ridiculous. Any competent jeweler would spot it as a fake in an instant." The old man reached up and tried to rub a kink out of his neck. "Mr. Barnes, you will forgive me if I say that I am not a well man. In fact, yours is probably one of the last commissions of a long and successful career. I shall soon retire to a comfortable chair and a pile of long neglected books. I don't mind telling you that I'd always hoped that the last of my work would be somewhat more . . . consequential."

"To copy a great stone is in itself a work of art, wouldn't you agree?" asked Barnes.

"Indeed, I would," said Herr Schulte. "Although copying your stone was similar to having a rather painful bowel movement."

"What did you say?" asked Barnes.

"I said that I am an old man near the end of life and that I am tired. Your bill is six thousand three hundred pounds. Your deposit was three thousand, so your balance is thirty-three hundred pounds. Will that be cash or charge?"

"It's the third largest pink diamond in the world."

"Yes, I know, bigger is always better, isn't that so?"

"You don't like the cut, is that it?"

"Please allow an old man to repair to his quilt and lonely cats, Mr. Barnes. I have done what you asked of me."

"What's wrong with it?" asked Barnes standing his ground.

"Nothing, nothing," said Schulte catching a labored breath. "Thirty-three hundred pounds if you please." The old lapidary artist began to cough, and Barnes noticed brown spittle escape the corner of his mouth.

"What would you have done with the stone, Mr. Schulte?"

The old man studied Barnes for a moment and took off his glasses to rub the bridge of his nose. "Since you have asked me, I will tell you. Not because I like you, but you are paying me a fair amount of money for a task I have performed well. In its present state - Famalah's Heart is an abomination. It is a monster. To a stonecutter with any sense of purity and balance, and it is nothing more than a billboard. It announces to the world that its owner wishes to have the biggest, if not the best, of everything.

The stone screams to be released from its garish prison to be seen as a true example of God's best work. True, it is flawless, but it is also tasteless. A much better scenario for the stone is to cut it into two identical pear-shaped works of art.

If I were commissioned to accomplish such a task, it would be the crowning achievement of a career devoted to the configuration of precious objects to their highest form.   And once my work was completed, I would name the stones after my precious wife whom God has chosen to place at His side until He decides the best time for me to join them.

That, Mr. Barnes, is what I would have done with the stone. Instead I have delivered you a very nice copy of your doorstop. If you would please pay for it and be on your way."

"What would be the value of the two stones together, Mr. Schulte?"

"Please don't belabor a moot point with a sick old man. I ask you to wave your carrot in front of another horse if you don't mind." The old man coughed again and had to sit down on a stool next to his work-bench.

"Would they bring more than the twenty-three million I paid for the one stone?" asked Barnes.

"If you sold them separately, no.   If they were perfectly identical and you sold them together, you could ask at least that much, probably much more."

"Is that a fact?"

~

There was a bitter sting to the icy wind off the ocean. Jerome Ripley couldn't believe his bad luck. *Easy does it,* he told himself.

He'd rappelled before in harsh conditions, so it shouldn't be too big of a deal. Still, the sheer height of the building was daunting. *Four hundred forty feet might be some kind of record*, he thought. His rappelling rope was four hundred and fifty feet long. His duffel bag would barely conceal it for the short walk to the parking lot and his car. The only evidence he needed to leave behind in the penthouse was the short section of *dynamic rope* wrapped around the bowl section of the toilet and the pulley that was attached to it, which was suspended just outside the bathroom window. The rappelling rope was *static* in nature, meaning that it would not stretch to absorb the shock of a fall. *Dynamic* rope is designed for that purpose. Since there was no actual climbing involved in the operation, the static rope was more than adequate for his needs.

After wrapping the smaller rope around the base of the toilet, Jerome fed the rappelling rope through the pulley and used a double cove hitch to tie a small iron pipe to the free end. This prevented the rope from passing back out through the pulley. Then he carefully lowered the other end of the long rope out the window all the way to the ground four hundred and forty feet below. This was the moment when he was beginning to take the most risk in the operation. The north side of the massive condominium was almost completely devoid of windows; however, every unit had a bathroom window in exactly the same location to facilitate the common water and sewer lines. This meant that as soon as Jerome lowered rope, there were forty potential witnesses if someone just happened to be using the bathroom at 3:15 A.M. Even though he parasailed onto the penthouse two hours earlier, and according to his instructions made sure that he spent at least ninety minutes inside, he waited until he thought all of people in the entire building were asleep to make his escape. He couldn't be sure with over four hundred units, but he was fortunate in that he could limit his exposure to only forty of them – and only for about fifteen minutes at that.

After the rappelling rope was in place, Jerome attached a two hundred-pound test mono-filament line, spooled around a Penn Senator fishing reel, to the iron pipe that was lodged with the cove hitches into the opening of the pulley. Then he gently lowered the fishing reel down the side of the building alongside the rappelling rope. Because the bathroom window was too small to admit the passage of his large shoulders, he made his way to the balcony that wrapped around the north side of the penthouse. It ran for over sixty feet on the east side that overlooked the ocean and then turned left and stretched out another eighteen feet along the north side. When he spotted the rope hanging out of the bathroom window about thirty feet away, Jerome was relieved to see that the stiff wind off of the ocean blew it toward the west and away from many of the bathroom windows below. Unfortunately, that same development made it all the more difficult to snag the line.

He had brought a collapsible fishing rod and an additional ultra-lightweight spinning reel filled with twelve-pound test mono-filament line for that purpose. At the end of the line were seven lead split-shots with a total weight of three-quarter's of an ounce. A foot past the split-shots at the very end of the line was a number 2 treble hook. It took almost nine minutes, a total of twenty-four casts, to catch the rappelling rope and draw it the over to the balcony. Then he had to connect his harness to the balcony railing using a forty-foot section of dynamic rope rigged through a second rappel device. His rappel devices were nothing more than small metal disks with oblong holes in their centers.   Both ropes were looped through a single carabiner fastened to his harness and then through the rappel devices and back up through the carabiner once more.   Then he tied off the static rappel rope to a fixed distance and used his leather gloved rappel hand to gradually pay out the dynamic rope until he was in a vertical position hanging thirty feet below the bathroom window.   It was then a simple matter to disengage his harness from the dynamic rope and release it to dangle from the balcony.   Then he could easily position himself off to the side of the bathroom windows in order to rappel off the side of the building all the way to the ground.   The whole descent took less than twenty minutes from beginning to end. When he reached the ground, he pulled down hard on the Penn Senator reel and disengaged the iron pipe from the pulley four hundred and forty feet above him.   Then he reeled in the thick monofilament line into the large fishing reel and pulled the rope through the pulley and down to the ground.   When the last bit of rope passed through the pulley, four hundred and forty feet of rope began a free fall and whistled through the air.   It piled up rapidly over a twenty foot area making a surprisingly loud noise like a fierce rainstorm against a skylight.

Remarkably, the sound went unnoticed by the people who occupied the ground unit. Blessing his good luck, Jerome quickly packed the huge pile of rope into his duffel bag and made his way all the way back to his car unnoticed.

Chapter One

By some stroke of luck I happen to be engaged to the world's most striking private detective. Her name is Martie Coleman. She has short, blond hair and hazel eyes. Her lean tall body is complemented with an attractive collection of slender features yet full sensuous lips. Her physical appearance is usually an asset to our agency, Willis & Coleman Investigations; however, I had to insist on working alone with the Palm Beach Police Department to set the stage for the recovery of Famalah's Heart for Heritage Insurance.

My name is Mack Willis, and I share a nice little house with Martie about an hour south of Palm Beach in a town called Deerfield Beach. She reluctantly agreed to steer clear of the Palm Beach Police Station until the final thrust of the investigation.

I magnanimously granted her the delivery because she gets such a kick out of it. It really doesn't make that big of a difference to me which one of us says, *"Gotcha!"* I'm just content to walk to the mailbox and retrieve the fat check that Heritage sends whenever we can manage to settle the claims against them. We usually get ten percent; however, Martie and I agreed to recover Famalah's Heart for two. After all, two percent of twenty-three million dollars is four hundred sixty thousand. Now, that's my idea of higher math.

I was told that Famalah's Heart is a fabulous stone. It's truly unique in that its seventeen-point-four carats facilitates a delightful heart shape, and it just happens to be the third largest pink diamond in the world. It was originally cut from a nineteen-carat raw pink diamond for Queen Famalah Pusahni-Shara of Tunisia. Her husband, King Bahnges Junabassi presented it to her for their fifth wedding anniversary. Queen Famalah was very honored to be given such a wonderful gift; however, she decided that it was much too lavish to keep.

Legend has it that the king, being well aware of his wife's humanitarian endeavors on behalf of her people, fully expected her to auction off the diamond and use the proceeds to procure medical supplies for the citizens of Tunisia. She would never miss the diamond. Her husband had given her many beautiful stones in the past.

They were the circumstances, which led to the arrival of the stone for auction at Christie's in London on the seventh of January, 2004. An American named Harold Barnes, who is the founder and CEO of Barnes Security Systems, Inc. out of Gloucester, Massachusetts, offered the winning bid of twenty-three million dollars. Mr. Barnes is presently a bachelor, so one would presume that being the owner of Famalah's Heart would make him the world's most eligible potential husband. The stone is too large for a ring setting, so it was held loosely in a pendant bezel by a braided, white gold wire.

The first thing Mr. Barnes did after procuring the diamond was to insure it with Heritage for the twenty-three million dollars. One of the provisions of the policy was that the location of the stone had to be documented at all times. The stone was treated as a separate entity, in and of itself, and it was held to a strict itinerary to be recorded with the company's headquarters during any change of location. Furthermore, it was further stipulated that the local law enforcement factions along any proposed route of travel were to be notified and supplied with the above-mentioned itinerary. Therefore, the stone was tracked at all times until it arrived in the safe located in Mr. Barnes's oceanfront condominium penthouse.

The name of Mr. Barnes's condo is called Stratos Club. It's a massive composition of glass, steel and concrete, which contains a total of four hundred and four units and encompasses eight hundred twenty thousand square feet of luxury living space. The first forty floors have ten – two thousand square foot units each, and the forty-first floor has four – five thousand square foot penthouses. Mr. Barnes owned the north penthouse for a winter get-a-way residence when he decided to stray from his native Brownsville, Texas.

On January eighth, the day after the auction at Christie's, Harold Barnes booked passage on the Queen Mary 2 from London to Port Everglades, Florida. He occupied the two thousand square foot executive suite for thirty-seven thousand dollars. Mr. Barnes traveled alone, but for some reason or another, he always required a huge amount of space. His cabin had its own private balcony and multi-media theatre.

Like most of the elements of Mr. Barnes's life, the journey back to America from London was a study in opulence. The suite boasted a private butler, personal chef and even a pillow concierge. There were nine pillows to choose from to insure the best possible night's sleep.

He rarely ventured outside the suite and kept in constant touch with the home headquarters of his security empire in New England. Barnes Security Systems, Inc. was spared Mr. Barnes's physical presence for six or eight months at a time. With his satellite-link computer network he could maintain a perpetual *hands-on* approach to management without ever leaving his houses. His employees resented the fact that he would never delegate any responsibility to them no matter how inconsequential. He wouldn't trust his engineers to purchase surveillance equipment without receiving demos by special courier, and he would never recognize any initiative shown by his employees to improve the efficiency of the corporation. Therefore, they never applied themselves to the task.

The employees never lasted very long at Barnes Security Systems, Inc. The money was adequate, but if a challenge or any attempt at attaining a sense of self-esteem were important, it was only a matter of time before the employees moved on. Mr. Barnes was oblivious to the situation. If he had his druthers, an employee number alone, instead of a name, would identify his staff.

It was rumored that was how he came to lose Famalah's Heart. He wouldn't trust his own security technicians to do the job they were well paid for. He had to do everything himself. Instead of changing his security code to a four-digit number of his choosing, he left the default sequence 4321 in place for too long. On one hand it was a leg up on the investigation because it meant that the thief had to be aware of the default code. However, narrowing down the number of people who were aware of the default code in Palm Beach was similar to obtaining a list of all the residents who kept valuable artifacts in their homes. It turned out to be approximately thirty-eight percent of the population.

Chapter Two

I met with the Heritage claims agents to go through the crime scene. Their lead man is named Bill Connally and he's a fairly nice guy. There's usually another guy named Peter Iris who follows him around. Bill met me at the private elevator for the north penthouse. "You're gonna' earn it this time, Mack," he said.

"Hey, Bill, Peter," I said as a greeting.

"You'll see that this guy was good," said Bill.

"They're all good, Bill. Until something breaks. What have you got so far?" I asked.

"Lets go on up. I'll fill you in." Bill Connally produced a key from his pocket and inserted it into the elevator lock. As the door opened he said, "Key operates the elevator. They're all private. Each penthouse gets their own. There's no keypad with a security code, no key - no go. There are only two keys – Barnes has one with him in Texas, and the security office had this one," he said holding it up.

"Anybody can copy a key," I told him.

"Not this key. It has a computer chip that has to be scanned by a receiver when you turn it. It's Barnes's own baby. His company installed them for all four penthouses."

"Okay, so you can't copy the key. What else you got?"

"The thief landed on the roof." He waited for my reaction. I was taking it all in and didn't respond right away. He continued, "Did you hear me?"

I parroted back for him, "The thief landed on the roof."

"That doesn't surprise you?" Peter asked.

"Not much surprises me anymore, Peter. Besides, why wouldn't he enter from the roof? Sounds like a good plan to me." The elevator had traveled up about twenty floors. The windows looking out over the parking lot revealed what an incredible height with which we were dealing.

Bill said, "It's forty-one floors, Mack. Over four-hundred feet."

"I'd say he started out considerably higher than that."

"Yeah, but still it's a pretty daring move. Plus, the wind was up. Somewhere about twenty knots," said Bill.

"It's a pretty big building, Bill. I'm not a skydiver, but if I were, I'll bet I could do it."

"We haven't gotten to the good part yet, Mr. Willis," said Peter. "Tell him, Bill."

"Hang on, Peter. A picture's worth a thousand words."

When we reached the landing for the north penthouse, the elevator doors slid open, and we found another set of locked doors. There were graphite stains where the fingerprint technicians had done their job, and Peter held up a second key that fit a handle set and a dead bolt lock that were clearly different than the lock that opened the elevator. "Too many locks," Peter said with conviction. "We don't think the thief was ever on the landing. He did the whole job from the roof and then left off the balcony."

"Peter, why don't you let Mr. Willis examine the crime scene all by himself," said Bill. "He used to be a policeman before he became an investigator, isn't that right, Mack?"

"I prefer the term, conga player, Bill. You know that."

"That's right, I almost forgot. What was the name of your last band?"

"I presume there was a safe?" I asked.

"In the bedroom. Behind a picture, as if that ever fooled anyone."

We entered Harold Barnes's penthouse and were assaulted by opulence. Oriental rugs, Chippendale chairs, you name it. There was a crystal chandelier in the dining room that had to have ten thousand prisms, which cast a million colored splinters of light around the ceiling until the sun's rays climbed above the adjacent picture window.

I felt fortunate that the whole experience was otherworldly to me. I could never live like that. Who would want to? The sheer arrogance of surrounding yourself with such lavish indulgences made you take an instant dislike of the owner.

Bill Connally led me over to one of the many sets of sliding doors. They all led to the massive balcony that overlooked the Atlantic Ocean. Once we stepped outside we could instantly see the benefit of living so high above the ground. The view was impressive. We had to look down on a squadron of pelicans flying in formation about a hundred feet below.

Peter pointed out the glass that had been neatly cut away and placed aside. The suction cups that were used to carry it were still attached. Again, the tell-tale evidence of the fingerprint tech was present.

"I'm sure they haven't found any prints," I guessed.

"Not a one," said Bill.

"Did he leave the parasail behind?" I asked.

"It's in the Palm Beach Police lab."

"I'm sure it was clean." I suggested.

"I don't know, yet," said Bill. "Should be."

"This guy was a pro. Is that what you're saying?" I asked rhetorically.

"Let's just say it probably wasn't Jerry Lewis."

"Naturally," I said. "He doesn't need the money."

"This guy was James Bond or something," said Peter Iris.

"Let me ask you the obvious question, Bill. If he left the parasail, how did he get to the ground?"

"Oh, you're gonna' love this," he said. "Follow me."

Chapter Three

Bill led me to the bathroom on the north side of the penthouse. The first thing I noticed was the rope wrapped around the base of the toilet. It was suspended off the floor and led to an open window where a set of vertical blinds were pulled to one side and rattling against the casing in the wind off the ocean. I asked him, "Doesn't that look a little strange to you, Bill."

"Of course, it does. How often do you see a rope hanging out a bathroom window?"

"But it's too small to fit through, isn't it?" I asked.

"We think he left by way of the balcony," said Peter.

"Why don't you give the man a chance," said Bill. "Come on out to the balcony and see what you think, Mack."

Bill led us out where the rope was tied to the railing on the north side of the balcony. I looked at the pulley that was attached to the rope hanging out of the bathroom window. I was getting a bit of vertigo looking over the edge. I asked Bill, "Is that about thirty feet to the window?"

"Just about. What do you think?" he asked me.

"I don't know," I admitted. "I guess he snagged the rope somehow and climbed down from here. I must say that this guy's pretty impressive. Talk about a second story man!"

"You think you can get a handle on this?" asked Peter Iris.

"No witnesses?"

"Uh uh," said Bill. "At least not yet."

"What about surveillance cameras?" I asked him.

"There aren't any on this side of the building."

"What about the next building over?"

"That's got to be at least five hundred feet, Mack."

"Well, if nothing else, maybe it'll give us the time of day. It's worth a try."

"Okay. Peter, will you do the honors?"

"You got it." Peter Iris left us to check out the security office in the building next door. With any luck the cameras might have gotten an image of the thief making his escape.

"What's missing from the safe? Have you talked to Barnes?"

"He's due in tonight from Texas. We know the diamond was stolen, but we're not sure what else was left in the safe."

"Twenty-three million? Who buys a diamond for twenty-three million, Bill?"

"Harold Barnes, for one. I'm sure it was just an investment. The guy is a real collector."

"I guess," I said. "You think he's in on it?"

"Man, I hope so. I hope you can catch him. Heritage can afford it, but twenty-three mill is a hell of a hit."

"I hear ya. I can use the finder's fee, too," I told him.

"Buys a lot of pizza, doesn't it, Mack?"

~

"Show me the safe," I asked him.

"It's a joke," said Bill.

"Don't tell me it's tin foil?" I asked.

"Just about."

"It doesn't wash, Bill. I did the background on this Barnes guy. He's in the business for God's sake, *the security business*."

"That's why you're here, man."

"Look around you. This guy buys the best of everything. Expensive furniture, rugs, oriental vases . . . now there's a curious development, Bill. Look behind you."

Bill Connally turned around, and I could see his jaw drop open, even from behind him, "Holy Mother of God! How did we miss that?" he asked.

"You know what it is, don't you?" I asked.

"It's big," he said.

"Yeah, but do you know the artist?" I asked him.

"I think it's a Monet," he said.

"Bingo."

"What's it worth?" asked Bill.

"You're the claims agent. What? You want me to do both our jobs?"

"It's got to be at least a couple mill. I don't get it," he said.

"I do."

"What?" asked Bill.

"Why didn't the thief take the painting? It would have been child's play. There's only one reason – he was told not to."

"But we can't prove that, Mack. We have to assume he was just after the diamond."

"Okay, but it sends us in the right direction. No thief in his right mind would pass up a Monet."

"Maybe he didn't know what it was," suggested Bill.

I just looked at him for a long moment.

"Okay, you win. Now what?"

"I'm going over to Palm Beach PD and get a few impressions. You call me when you hear back from Peter. You got my number?"

"You going back to Deerfield Beach tonight?" he asked.

"If you met my new girl, you wouldn't have to ask."

"Good for you. At least somebody's getting some."

"What ever happened to Mrs. Connally?" I asked.

"Oh, she's still there," he said. "That's why I don't get any." We both got a laugh out of that.

Chapter Four

The Palm Beach Police Chief is a very handsome woman. She has very smooth cocoa-colored skin and wears the gray on her head like a badge of wisdom. To hear her tell it, she has earned every strand of gray hair making sure that the citizens of Palm Beach are protected against crime and that her position is protected against any semblance of tokenism. Evangeline Brooks leaves her considerable feminine powers at home each morning. She has to lead a very busy squad room.

We had met before on a number of other occasions, and I was looking forward to the chance to work with her again.

"Hello, Mack," she began. "How's the world treating you?"

"I'm hangin' in there, chief." I told her.

"The door's closed, Mack. Did you forget my name?"

"You know I didn't Evangeline. How have you been?"

"I'm getting worn out if you want to know the truth."

"You don't look it," I said honestly.

"Always the charmer. Are you going to catch this Barnes with his hand in the honey pot?" she asked.

"You bet."

"Where are you going with it now?"

"I haven't the slightest."

"Pretty confident, aren't we, Mack?"

"Oh, I don't know. It never hurts to have faith. I get to be wrong now and then. I just don't get paid."

"What's the commission?" she asked.

"Two percent," I told her. I watched her do the math in her head.

"Hoo-wee! You know I'm still single, right?"

"Believe me, Evangeline, I'll keep it in mind."

The chief assembled all of the detectives in the squad room the next morning. I could tell by some of the tired faces that some of them worked the night shift and wanted to go home and hit the hay. For their sake I meant to be brief, but I wanted to play out a little fishing line and see if I could catch something, "Thank you all for coming. My name is Mack Willis, and you all know why I'm here. I'm sure you are capable of discovering who stole the diamond from The Stratos."

"What diamond?" asked a young African American with loose fitting clothes and a large gold earring beneath his Rasta curls.

"Chief Brooks, haven't your detectives been informed of the contents of Barnes' safe?" I asked.

"Some of them have, Mr. Willis," she said. "Detective Ripley is just finishing his shift. The purpose of this meeting is to get us all on the same page."

"Some things don't add up just yet," I began, "and I'd like to bounce them off of you to chew on for a while. As some of you have learned, a large diamond was stolen from a Mr. Harold Barnes's north-side penthouse of the Stratos Club. It was insured by Heritage Insurance, Ltd. out of London, England, for twenty-three million dollars. I have met with their stateside affiliates who have been very cooperative – giving us all of the information at their disposal.

The theft was discovered by the owners of the condominium unit directly below Mr. Barnes' penthouse. Mr. and Mrs. Michael

Stamos found a rope hanging down onto their balcony and called the Stratos Club security office. They in turn notified Heritage Insurance and The Palm Beach Police Department. As far as we know, the diamond was the only thing of value taken. That in itself is suspicious in my mind and further questions remain as to the M.O. of the thief. Would anyone like to begin a discussion of possible suspects?" I asked.

"Barnes did it," said one of the men.

"He stole his own diamond for the insurance money," said another.

"Okay, let's say Barnes did it. How was it done?" I asked.

"He paid someone to open the safe and take some cash and other valuables," said Detective Ripley.

"Very good," I told him. "How did he get into the penthouse?"

"He flew in on a parasail," said another detective.

"What is your name, Detective?" I asked him.

"Hector Ramero, at your service."

"Detective Ripley, tell detective Romero why the thief didn't use the parasail to get to the ground?"

"Scuse me?" Ripley said.

"Well, the thief used a parasail to get onto the roof of the penthouse, right?"

"Yeah, so?"

"How did he get to the ground?"

"By rappelling down the side of the building," said Ramero.

"Exactly. He even left footprints down the side of the building as well as some of his climbing gear attached to a balcony and a toilet. Pretty sloppy, wouldn't you say?"

"But no fingerprints," said Ramero.

"True," I said, "but he may have been recorded by a security camera next door."

"What?" said Ripley. "I didn't know that The Stratos Club had any security cameras on the north side."

"A man named Peter Iris is checking it out as we speak, Detective Ripley." I wasn't lying, even though I knew that Peter would probably come up empty. "The security tape might be able to give us some clues as to the thief's identity." I planted a seed of doubt. Maybe if I waited long enough something might sprout. The detectives began to discuss the possibilities as to why the thief used a rope to reach the ground. I waited patiently pretending to look over my notes. One of them spoke up, "Is it true that a lot of valuable artifacts were left behind?"

"Yes, it is. One item in particular is an original Monet painting worth millions," I told them.

"Something stinks," said one of the men.

"That's what I thought. It seems to me that the thief was leaving a calling card behind. If he used the parasail to reach the ground, then he wouldn't have had to leave any ropes or footprints behind. Plus, his escape would have been that much faster."

"Maybe four-hundred forty feet is not high enough to use the parasail," suggested one of the detectives.

"That's a really good question, and one I hope to have answered by this time tomorrow. I'd also like to know just how much an industrial drill and an oxy-acetylene torch weighs. The thief had to jump from a plane with a lot of heavy equipment." There were more murmurs around the room.

"That man was crazy," said Ripley.

"Or hungry," I suggested.

"You ain't hungry when you're dead," said Ripley.

"Has anyone here had any experience using a parasail or parachute?"

No one spoke up. "How about climbing? Has anyone used a rappel device or done any rock climbing?" Again no one spoke up. "Okay, would anyone like to do the research?"

"I'll do it," said Ripley. Somehow I felt that he would. I was almost positive that the theft was an inside job of some sort. Barnes had commissioned someone to rob his penthouse, but the diamond wasn't there. He would never trust anyone with a stone of that value. I felt sure that the stone had never even made it to Palm Beach in the first place. Unfortunately, I hadn't the slightest idea how to prove it. I thanked the men in the squad room for their input and drove back to Martie in Deerfield Beach.

Chapter Five

Martie met me at the door with a drink and her notes. She had been on the internet researching diamonds, parasailing, and rock climbing. It's nice to have a clever fiancée. She told me, "Mack, this could get expensive for you having me look at all these diamonds."

"I've already given you a ring. One ring per marriage if I'm not mistaken."

"Some rapper just bought his main squeeze a pair of twenty-four million dollar earrings."

"You're kidding?"

"She must be *great* in bed." she said.

"She probably witnessed a murder."

"Always the romantic, huh, Mack?"

"I'm just being practical. Who would buy his girlfriend a pair of twenty-four million dollar earrings?"

"Sounds like a very nice guy to me."

"Tell me that you'd rather have a stinking rapper than me?" I asked her.

"I'm thinking, I'm thinking."

"Very funny. I happen to know that you can't stand rap music."

"I'll learn to like it."

"All I can say is that you probably deserve each other."

"Thanks a lot," she said laughing.

"Where were the diamond earrings purchased?" I asked. She picked up a newspaper and read, *"AMSTERDAM American rapper Q Z Bad recently purchased a pair of pear shaped diamond earrings with a total weight of sixteen carats. The pink gems are identical, flawless diamonds and are reportedly worth every bit of their twenty-three million nine hundred thousand-dollar price tag, plus tax.*

Apparently the rapper has a sense of humor regarding the exorbitant cost of the gems and has changed their name from Angelina's Tears to The Tears of Q Z Bad. The couple are expected to wed sometime in the spring."

"She better marry him," I said.

"What did you find out about the climbing equipment?" I asked.

"Well, first of all, four-hundred-fifty feet of static rope weighs about ninety-five pounds."

"Jesus."

"That's not all. Add the sixty pounds of an industrial drill and even a small oxy-acetylene tank, plus the weight of an average man and you're up to three hundred ninety pounds. That's a lot of weight for a parasail to support. As far as I can tell, it's possible, but the descent rate would be about thirty percent faster than normal. In addition to that, the flare-out would be much more critical to accomplish with any accuracy."

"What the hell's a flare-out."

"Oh, you've seen it. It's that move that slows down the parasailor and arrests his descent for just an instant. It's when they pull down on the ropes at the last minute."

"It could be done, right?"

"Yup," she said.

"Well, that's all that Barnes needed. I'm sure that the rope and drill were already waiting for the thief in the penthouse the night of the robbery."

"What makes you say that?" she asked.

"Simple. All Barnes needs is a plausible scenario for the crime. He wouldn't make his burglar carry all that weight. He just brought it upstairs a little at a time. The torch during one trip, and the ropes, pulley and rappelling devices during another one."

"What's our next move?" she asked.

"I think we need to crack a safe."

"What?"

"I want to do just what the thief did."

"What do you know about cracking a safe? Were you a thief in a past life or something?"

"Hey, how hard can it be?"

"Somehow I think I'm gonna' find out."

Chapter Six

We called Barnes Security, Inc. the next day to find out how to violate Harold Barnes' safe. His model was called the 1200-E, which designates the total weight and the fact that it's the fifth in a series. The only improvements with each successive model were the materials used. The 1200-F is a carbon steel and tungsten alloy, which is twenty percent larger than the E model. The difference being that while the metal is lighter to facilitate the larger size, it is also a great deal stronger. Fortunately for Martie and me, the 1200-E is only made of ordinary stainless steel. It's only intended to slow a thief down and is by no means foolproof. I found it curious that a man who owns a company that installs safes and usually buys the best of everything used his bargain basement model for his own home. I called Bill on his cell, "We're going to need an industrial drill exactly like the one left at the scene and a one inch diamond tipped boring bit. Plus, we'll also need an oxy-acetylene torch."

"That sounds expensive," he said.

"It's about six hundred give or take."

"What's it for?"

"The safe, naturally."

"I guessed that much, Mack, but why?"

"We want to know how long it takes to bore the hole into the safe and cut off the hinges."

"Who's we? You got a mouse in your pocket?"

"You get to meet Martie. Believe me, it's a good thing," I told him.

"I could use a good thing right about now. Where do you want to meet?"

"I'll need access to the penthouse anyway, so why don't you meet us there?"

"Sounds good," he said.

"How did Peter make out with the surveillance tape?"

"It's a no go. They have tapes, but not of that side of the building. I guess they figure that all the bad guys will enter through the front door."

"They may be right."

"I hear ya'. Is it okay if I bring Peter along? He's dying to meet your new girl."

"Sure, why not. How does 3:00 P.M. sound?"

"You sure I can fill your order by then?"

"All you have to do is pick it up. It's at Hughes Industrial Supply on old Dixie, right in the heart of West Palm."

"You said six hundred?"

"That's just the drill bit," I told him.

"Ouch."

I stopped off at the Palm Beach Police Station to check in

with Jerome Ripley, who was nice enough to volunteer to get some information on skydiving and rock climbing for the investigation. He was following up a lead on another case he was working, but he had left a folder for me at the front desk. I took the folder to the Palm Beach Holiday Inn where Martie had rented us a room. I found her in the restaurant. "I just can't imagine how you keep your shape, Martie. I've never seen a person eat five meals a day and not gain an ounce."

"I've got a high metabolism. What can I say?"

"I'm just jealous. I can eat a pretzel and it'll show up on my gut."

"More to love, that's all."

"I'm glad you feel that way. I got a folder from Jerome."

"You think he's on our side?"

"The jury's still out on that one."

"He seems to be anxious to contribute."

"*Seems* is the operative word in that sentence."

"I thought you were going to work on that cynicism of yours, Willis."

"If I do, we might starve to death."

"You could always start the band up again. What were you guys called again?"

"You want to hear what Jerome has to say?"

"Lay it on me," she said.

"Jerome was very helpful, actually. He has determined that eight out of ten respondents said that they could easily jump off a building four-hundred-forty feet high. It apparently is no big deal for an experienced skydiver. According to his notes, some of the skydivers have jumped off of buildings almost half that high. Anything over three hundred feet is easily doable.

Again the question remains why would a person go through the trouble to make his escape down the building by means of a rope and a rappel device? There was only one reason and it stared us in the face. Someone wanted to leave the tell-tale signs that the building was violated and they traveled clumsily to the ground on the   outside of the building.

I'd seen a lot of burglary scenes in my eighteen years in law enforcement, but I'd never seen anything so blatantly obvious. That in itself was not anything that could get Heritage off the hook. I had to get a "chink in the armor" so to speak. Barnes Security, Inc. was more than helpful. They seemed to enjoy the irony of the situation. I was informed exactly how one would go about cracking a 1200-E series safe using a diamond tipped drill-bit and an oxy-acetylene torch. It was interesting to note that had I not had that information, I doubt that I would have been able to do it. A one-inch hole had to be drilled exactly half-way down the hinge-side seam to sever the back-bolt. The three fore-bolts were left in place and both of the hinges had to be sheared off with the torch. Then a simple putty knife in the hinge-side seam could pry the door open far enough to back the fore-bolts away from the housing. The whole process took about an hour. Since the safe was already purged, Martie and I drilled a second hole on the hinge-side seam right below the first one. Then we re-cut the hinge brackets just to determine how long it would take.

We bagged the steel filings produced by the diamond drill-bit just as the crime scene technicians had done. I gave the torch and drill back to Bill just in case he'd like to give them to his wife for

Christmas next year. Personally, I don't know why he bothers. She never even used the chainsaw that he gave her last year. Martie asked me, "What have you got cooking, Mack?"

"Interesting choice of words," I told her. "It is actually cooking indeed."

"What's cooking?" she asked.

"Not much, what's cooking with you?" I asked her.

"I guess I walked right into that one," she frowned.

"Yes, you did."

Chapter Seven

The next time I met with Jerome Ripley he asked if the information in the folder was any help to me. "You bet," I told him. "Sounds like any x-games sports nut would really enjoy jumping off a building as high as the Stratos Club. They'd do it for kicks if they could get away with it."

"Yeah, so?" he asked.

"Well, what does that tell you, Jerome?"

"How am I supposed to know?" he asked.

"You're not supposed to *know*. You're supposed to *think*."

"Oh, well, maybe the brothers aren't as smart as you white detectives, ever think of that?"

"That's bullshit, Jerome, and you know it."

"Mebbe I spose ta' know because the brother guilty. Is that what you saying?"

"What have you got a guilty conscious or something?"

"You racist, man."

"Oh, horseshit, detective. I'm a musician for God's sake. I have been for over twenty years. If there's one sure thing that a musician isn't, it's a racist. I've been playing gigs with black dudes since you were in diapers."

"That don't mean nothin'. You racist!" he insisted.

"Yeah, okay, knock yourself out, I'm a racist."

"And what you doin' makin' eyes at 'Vangeline fo. She don't need yo' whitebread ass."

"You mean Chief Brooks?" I asked pointedly. "You need to learn a little respect for your superiors." I told him. Just then Chief Brooks entered the room and Detective Ripley turned to her and said, "He a racist."

"He *is* a racist, Jerome," corrected Chief Brooks.

"No, I'm not," I said.

"I know you're not, Mack," said Evangeline, "I just thought I'd start my day by beating a dead horse." She glared at Ripley.

"Say what?" asked Detective Ripley.

"Never mind, Jerome," said the chief. Man, she really looked attractive when she was angry.

Ripley said to me, "I know I seen you somewhere, man."

"Yeah, I've been around for a while."

"Mack and I go way back," said Evangeline.

"I'll bet you do," said Ripley.

"Just what are you implying, Detective?" asked the chief to her subordinate.

"I just agree'n wit chew dat's all," he said. "I know I seen you somewhere, it'll come to me."

"I can't wait," I told him. He glared at me with his coal black shiny eyes, and I felt my life passing before mine for just an instant.

"Yeah, you da' man, for now," he said and walked out of the room.

Evangeline felt that she had to apologize for Detective Ripley. "Forget it," I told her. "Assholes come in all colors."

Chapter Eight

I drove down to Del Ray Beach to the office of the Broward County Coroner. A Forensic Pathologist named Jim Bailey met with me, and we discussed the feasibility of taking photographs of the steel filings from the safe with an electron microscope. He said it could be done, but questioned who would pay for the procedure. Jim was a nice guy, but he had to answer to a bunch of bean counters just like all the other county employees. I told him he could bill Heritage Insurance, Ltd. and he told me it shouldn't be a problem. When he asked for the filing samples, I told him that they were still in the police lab up in Palm Beach and I would drop them off in about twenty-four hours. Then I drove back to the Palm Beach Holiday Inn where Martie was waiting to go out to dinner.

We chose a little bistro called *The Banana Boat* right on the Intra-coastal Waterway. Coincidentally, our waiter Jake remembered me from about two years back when I was playing in a band that did a gig there. He asked me, "What ever happened to you guys?"

"Oh, you know, the usual," I told him. "Somebody's girlfriend broke up the band. No wait," I said, "Now that you mention it, it was the other way around. The lead singer's boyfriend broke us up if I remember correctly. Claimed she was never around when he needed her."

"What was the name of the band again? Something about a rash or something?"

"Jake, tell me what's good?" I asked him. "We should stick to seafood, right?"

"Oh, man, it's killer," Jake said.

Martie ordered some conch chowder and a Caesar salad, and I had a blackened mahi and yellowtail tuna combo. It was great. I'm still wearing it on my gut to this day, but Martie worked off her dinner walking back to the car.

The next morning over coffee, Martie noticed that I had placed the stainless steel filings that we had produced in the penthouse on a saucer by the open sliders.

"Has that door been open all night?" she asked.

"Yup." I told her.

"You left it open on purpose?"

"That's right," I said.

"But you have the air-conditioning on. Let me guess - you're trying to combat global warming."

"Every little bit helps."

~

Later that afternoon I drove over to the station house and asked Evangeline for a small sample of the steel filings that her lab technicians removed from the robbery scene. "What's up, Mack?" she asked. "You onto something?"

"I hope so, but I'm not sure just yet. Believe me, Evangeline, if I'm right, you'll be the first to know."

Chapter Nine

Harold Barnes got in from Brownsville, Texas, at about four in the afternoon. He met with Bill Connally and Peter Iris about processing his claim. They told him that things were moving forward and that if the stone was not recovered in a week's time, they were authorized to cut him a check.

I dropped off the filing samples to Jim Bailey just before he was leaving for the day. I asked him to make sure that they remained sealed until right before he photographed them with the electron microscope. They were labeled exhibit A and exhibit B according to when they were gathered. Exhibit B was the sample that I had left out in the night salt air at the Holiday Inn. Exhibit A was the sample bagged by the lab technicians the day after the thief had rappelled down the side of the Stratos Club.

Martie and I were awakened the next day with some gruesome and unexpected news. Jerome Ripley's was found dead in his apartment, apparently shot in the head with a small twenty-five caliber handgun. The gun was left at the scene, and there were no fingerprints. There was no sign of forced entry and nothing in the apartment had been disturbed. His wallet was still in his back pocket with two-hundred eighty dollars inside. "It wasn't robbery," I said to Evangeline.

"No, it wasn't."

"Any ideas?" I asked her.

"You know what I'm thinking, Mack. Don't make me say it."

"I know, Evangeline. It always hurts to suspect that one of your guys is dirty."

"Shit," she said. "Barnes is gonna' win, isn't he?"

"Maybe not. Don't give up hope. Have you sealed up Ripley's apartment?"

"Of course," she said. "I just hope we can find something to tie him to Barnes."

"I'm sure Barnes is no dope. It won't be anything obvious like a letter or anything. You better count on forensics."

"Talk about a needle in a haystack," she said.

"More like a Caucasian hair in a Rasta guy's house."

Jim Bailey produced a couple of beautiful photographs later that same day. They clearly showed that the two samples were very different with respect to the amount of oxidation produced by exposure to salt air off the Atlantic Ocean. Since the first sample was bagged the day after the robbery, the oxidation duration should have been limited to twenty-four hours. However, the photographs showed that the filings were severely corroded compared to the sample that I produced at the Holiday Inn. Therefore, it could be concluded that the hole had been drilled in Barne's safe before he ever left for Brownsville, Texas. It was determined that the filings had been lying in front of the safe for at least two weeks.

Heritage Insurance was subsequently let off the hook for the insurance claim because his safe was effectively left open. That was a clear violation of the terms of the policy – lack of diligence to protect the security of the stone. Bill Connally was thrilled to write Martie and me a check for four-hundred-sixty thousand dollars.

Chapter Ten

When I brought Martie to the Palm Beach Police Station to meet Evangeline, she asked me if we were ever lovers. I told her, "Not a chance. Evangeline has too much class to date a guy like me."

"Thanks a lot, Mack," she said in a huff. "I guess I'm just a shameless hussy."

"I wouldn't say that. You have plenty of shame."

"If you break my heart, Willis. I swear to God I'll shoot you in the ass."

When Evangeline met Martie, she took me aside and said, "She's lovely, Mack. I can see now that I never had a chance."

"I'm a lucky man, Evangeline."

"Just don't you forget it."

Evangeline called us about three weeks later and told us of Harold Barnes' arrest. It couldn't have happened to a nicer guy. They found his hair in Ripley's apartment, and Ripley's hair in his penthouse. They also found the copy of Famalah's heart that Ripley had taken during the robbery hidden in a container of pink grapefruit juice.

As far as the real Famalah's Heart is concerned, I'm pretty sure that it became a set of earrings called The Tears of Q Z Bad. I got the idea from Martie's comment that I'd better not break her heart.

Evangeline met us for lunch the next day back at the Banana Boat. She told me the charges against Barnes were sure to stick. He would be charged with insurance fraud as well as Detective Ripley's murder. She also surprised me with a bit of information that I wished she would have passed along in private. "Ripley finally remembered where he knew you from. He told me that he once saw you performing in a band called *Painful Burning Feminine Itch.*"

"Oh, Mack," said Martie shaking her head.

"Hey, what can I say? We were fly."

The End

www.ingramcontent.com/pod-product-compliance
Lightning Source LLC
Chambersburg PA
CBHW060401260626
47160CB00006B/2388